THE COMMISSIONER
The most HUGELY important person in the **Future Perfect Unit** *.

LANGLEY VON TINKLEHORN
The greatest Time Crime Catcher the World has EVER seen.

GUSSAGE ST VINCENT
Silver-toothed Time Pirate - and all round bad egg.

* The **Future Perfect Unit** (FPU) is a top secret, and super-hush-hush government organization set up in 2509 to combat illegal TIME-TRAVEL activity.

The FUTURE AGENT RESEARCH training school for those who

Prologue

WARNING!
WARNING!
WARNING!

I'm going to be honest with you.

The journey that you are about
to embark on is rather
complicated.

And when I say "rather"
I mean "unbelievably"
and when I say
"complicated"
I mean
"C·O·M·P·L·I·C·A·T·E·D".

Some things
are about to
HAPPEN
that could very well
alter not only the
DESTINY
OF HUMANITY,
but also
SHAPE THE
FUTURE
OF THE
ENTIRE
UNIVERSE.

Bearing ALL THIS in

mind

and with one thing and another
and the price of fish going up
and so forth, I wanted to try and make

LIFE

a little bit simpler.
So, to AVOID too much

unnecessary confusion

I thought it'd be best for ALL
concerned if we took a look

first at where everything

BEGAN...

Compton Valance:
THE FUTURE
So Far

Compton Valance and Bryan Nylon are two ten-year-old boys who, thanks to a series of **HIGHLY IMPROBABLE EVENTS** too ridiculous to bore you with here, accidentally created a **TIME MACHINE** out of a mouldy cheese-and-pickled-egg sandwich.

Not long afterwards, Compton and Bryan met a **top-secret, TIME-TRAVELLING agent** from **600 years** in **THE FUTURE** called Samuel Nathaniel Daniels.

The boys used the stinky sandwich to travel backwards and forwards through time, and save **THE UNIVERSE** from certain **DESTRUCTION**. Compton and Bryan were then invited by the **most important** person of the **twenty-seventh century**, the **Commissioner** of the **Future Perfect Unit**, to train to become **TIME-TRAVELLING agents** themselves.

They have just completed their **first** term of **training** at the **F. A. R. T. Academy**, during which they managed to **foil** an attempt to **steal** the **TIME MACHINE SANDWICH** by Gussage St Vincent

(the **most DASTARDLY** and **fancily-trousered** time **crim*** in the world).

* A Time Crim is a person who illegally TRAVELS THROUGH TIME without the knowledge or permission of the **FPU**.

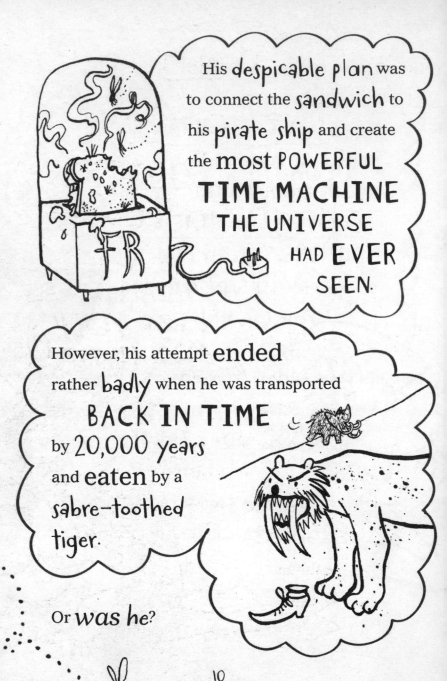

His **despicable plan** was to connect the **sandwich** to his **pirate ship** and create the **most POWERFUL TIME MACHINE THE UNIVERSE HAD EVER SEEN.**

However, his attempt **ended** rather **badly** when he was transported **BACK IN TIME** by **20,000 years** and **eaten** by a **sabre-toothed tiger.**

Or **was he?**

Chapter 1

The Fearless Bandit (Fastest Slinger in Town)

COMPTON VALANCE! I'M A-COMIN' FOR YOU!

The Fearless Bandit sat on top of his ENORMOUS METAL hover-horse and shouted his terrible threat.

On the other side of Main Street, Compton flexed his fingers and turned to look at his best friend, Bryan Nylon.

What do you think, Bry? Can we take him?

Unfortunately, Bryan was way too busy to listen, as he was attempting to see if he could sneak up on his own ears by twisting his head to the side as quickly as possible.

Compton turned back and watched as his dastardly opponent, THE MOST WANTED OUTLAW IN THE GALAXY, climbed down from his mighty, floating steed and moved himself into battle position. A single bead of sweat trickled from Compton's forehead and slowly traced a path down the side of his face.

A lone howl from a distant hound and the weird whistling noise that Bryan made when he breathed in and out through his nose were the only sounds to cut through the SILENCE.

You may begin firing on the twelfth bell of noon, gentlemen,

said the ROBOT SHERIFF, pointing to the town's laser-clock display.

BONG!

And NOT a moment sooner,

he added, before squeaking off to hide behind a HUGE water barrel.

BONG! Compton took a **DEEP BREATH** and readied himself.

BONG!

He stepped forwards, dimly aware of the townsfolk peering anxiously from behind the safety of their front doors, hoping beyond hope that someone would rid their town of The Fearless Bandit

BONG! once and for ALL. Compton narrowed his eyes and focused his gaze on his opponent at the other end of Main Street, all the time studying him for a flicker of weakness.

BONG!

The Fearless Bandit STARED BACK at Compton. His face may have been hidden beneath a black mask,

but Compton could see **evil** glinting
and twinkling **DEEP** within his eyes.

BONG!

The Bandit's
outrageous
moustache
billowed and fluttered
in the **swirling**
wind and, when
he smiled,
two rows of
silver teeth
sparkled
like
DIAMONDS
in the noonday sun.

BONG! Compton took another step forwards. He was now standing directly behind his **regulation pie table**. It **groaned** under the weight of the **custard pies** it was carrying.

Never **once** **BONG!** taking his eyes off his **enemy**, Compton let his fingers gently feel their way around the lip of a pie crust. With a deft **flick** of his wrist, he held the **custardy treat** in the palm of his hand. The move was **quick** and **instinctive**. The pie was now an extension of his own body.

BURP

BONG!

Bryan tried to see how many times he could make himself burp between BONGS. His record was twelve.

BONG! Compton tensed his arm muscles, ready to launch a custard pie at his mortal enemy, and waited for the last tolls of the noonday bell.

"Get ready, Bry," he said turning to his friend.

Bry? Bry-an?

Bryan had VANISHED from next to the pie table and was now sitting inside the town's jail cell.

BONG!

"W-w-what's *happening*?" said Compton in a state of high confusion. "How did you…?"

SPLAT!

A HUGE pie caught Compton full in the face and whacked him backwards.

SPLAT! Before he had a chance to react, another pie hit him in the chest, knocking him to the ground. Compton heard people booing and jeering as he turned round to appeal to the ROBOT SHERIFF.

"No fair!" he pleaded, spitting sweet custard out of his mouth. "He didn't wait for the twelfth bell."

SPLAT!!

Another pie caught him on the side of the head.

"BRYAN!" he yelled, as a torrent of custard and pastry rained down on him. "BRYAN!" Through the sticky yellow gloop running down his face, Compton looked at Bryan in the town's jail. Bryan looked back for a moment and then turned into a GIANT blancmange and started eating himself.

BRYAN!

Compton suddenly awoke with a start and sat straight up in his bed.

BRYAN!

he called, his garbled shout dying on the air.

He looked around and breathed a big sigh of relief when he saw that he was in his bedroom, in Morlock Cottage, in Little Hadron. It had been a dream, a stupid, crazy DREAM. He felt his forehead – it was damp with sweat, so he threw back his duvet to cool himself down.

This was not the first time the ENORMOUSLY moustached, silver-toothed and DESPICABLE Fearless Bandit had stalked Compton in his sleep. No, Compton had dreamed about him almost EVERY night for the last twelve weeks. As he lay in his bed, his breathing slowly returning to normal, he couldn't help but wonder whether his bad dreams were connected to the incidents of three months earlier.

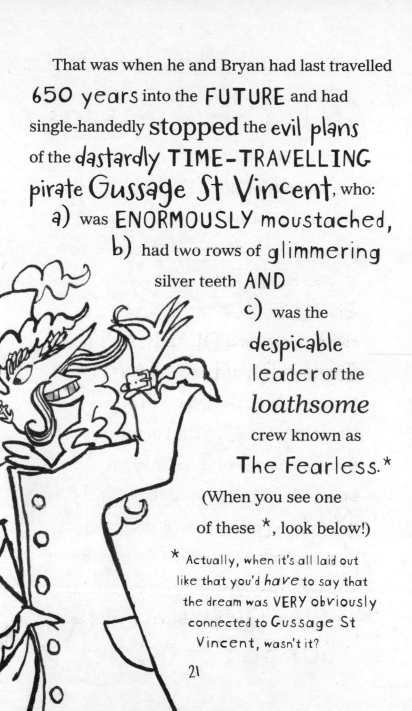

That was when he and Bryan had last travelled 650 years into the FUTURE and had single-handedly stopped the evil plans of the dastardly TIME-TRAVELLING pirate Gussage St Vincent, who:

a) was ENORMOUSLY moustached,

b) had two rows of glimmering silver teeth AND

c) was the despicable leader of the loathsome crew known as The Fearless.*

(When you see one of these *, look below!)

* Actually, when it's all laid out like that you'd *have* to say that the dream was VERY obviously connected to Gussage St Vincent, wasn't it?

21

Chapter 2

<u>ABOLISH Tuesdays</u>

Compton wiped the sleep from his eyes
and looked at his bedside clock. It said

TUESDAY
07:00

"Tuesday," he moaned. "Not Tuesday,
anything but <u>TUESDAY</u>!"

Compton had only been in

Year 6 for a few weeks but he

already loathed Tuesdays.

In fact, he looked forward to

Tuesdays about as much as a

prawn looks forward to an

ALL-YOU-CAN-EAT
SEAFOOD
BUFFET.

Tuesday was the day when Compton's horrific science teacher, **Strictly Strickland**, forced his class to endure the most **BRAIN-NUMBING HOUR in the HISTORY of EVER**.

And today, Compton felt even **less** like Strickland's **sixty-minute bore attack** than usual, because something **heavier** than an **ENORMOUS elephant** sitting on top of **another even more ENORMOUS elephant** was weighing on his mind.

It was now early October, and nearly **three months** since his last trip to the **twenty-seventh century.** In fact, since completing **PHASE ONE TRAINING** at the **F. A. R. T. Academy**, he hadn't heard a **peep** out of **anyone** at the **FPU.** Every single day since he and Bryan had returned from the year **2664,** the subject of when they would go back and begin **PHASE TWO TRAINING** was **all** either of them could think about.

"When's **Samuel Nathaniel Daniels** going to get in touch?" Compton **sighed** to himself as he clambered out of bed and began to get ready for school.

Compton was quickly **realizing** that one of the **biggest** drawbacks of being a **time traveller** without your own **TIME-TRAVEL MACHINE** was having to rely on communications with a **highly forgetful man** in a tight silver suit from *over six* centuries in the FUTURE (*#27thCenturyProblems*).

As he buttoned up his school shirt, Compton thought about how ordinary and straightforward his LIFE had once been. It *used* to be full of things that everyone else does, like:

going to school...

or playing in the park...

or seeing how many farts you can fit in a tent.

In fact, LIFE had been full of regular, normal stuff right up until the day before his tenth birthday. That was the day that he and Bryan discovered that they had created a sandwich that was capable of sending them

travelling through time.

Since that moment, Compton's life had become stranger than a chicken wearing a nappy.

For instance, there was that time sixty-six million years ago when he and Bryan had made the dinosaurs extinct with the help of a packet of custard creams.

Then there was that time when his **dad** had

← turned into a **woman**.

Then there was that time when they SAVED **THE UNIVERSE** from being **destroyed** by Compton's older brother, **Bravo**. ➝

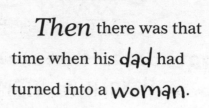

The thing was, Compton

loved his **new** and **improved**, jam-packed-to-the-top-of-the-jar kind of life. It was full of adventure and **excitement** and adventure and **thrills** and adventure and spills and adventure and adventure. All he wanted to do was get **back**, er, well, **forwards**, to the **twenty-seventh** century and begin the next **PHASE** of his training to become a fully fledged **FPU Agent**,

travel backwards and forwards through **TIME**

and maybe, just *maybe*,

HELP SAVE THE WORLD AGAIN.

It was precisely because he wanted it SO much that **not** hearing *anything* from Samuel Nathaniel Daniels was so difficult. However, ALL that was about to **change**. At the **exact same moment** that Compton was getting ready to leave for school, **LIFE** itself was holding a **great BIG** jug of adventure and was about to pour it all over his face.

Chapter 3

Three Minutes into the Most BRAIN-NUMBING HOUR in the HISTORY of EVER

The air in the science classroom of
St Geoffrey's Junior School
was warm and **thick**, as
Strickland droned on and on...
and on and on and on and on...
As usual, today's lesson with
Strictly Strickland was even
more boring than a
GIGANTIC mole.

29

Compton **looked** over at Bryan, who was **so bored** that he was holding open his **eyelids** with his thumbs and forefingers, and he **wasn't** the only one either. **Barry Wales**'s head kept **nodding** forwards every few moments as he fought the urge to **fall asleep.** ZZZ ZZZZ ZZZZ...

Allan Exit was doing some **HEAVY-DUTY**, level-ten, black-belt **deep breathing** to try and stay **focused.** Even **Margo Lugg,** a girl who **usually** put her hand up to answer **EVERY** single question **correctly,** had an expression on her face like a **constipated gibbon.**

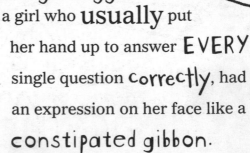

Only **three minutes** had passed since the beginning of the lesson and there were still **another fifty-seven** to go. **Fifty-seven minutes!** Compton simply **didn't** think he'd be able to make it.

It was then, when **all hope** seemed lost, a **knock** at the classroom door interrupted Strictly Strickland's gravitational flow.

COME IN!

he **barked,** ready to give whoever had **dared disrupt** his lesson a **LARGE** slice of **angry pie.** The door s l o w l y creaked open to reveal a short, **PLUMP** man wearing a **HUGE** overcoat **on top** of another **HUGE** overcoat **on top** of a **wetsuit** that looked **painfully** small.

The whole EXTRAORDINARY look was topped off with a pair of fishing waders and a diving mask and snorkel. Compton looked excitedly at Bryan.

Er, y-y-yes?

spluttered

Strickland, clearly

taken aback by the

astonishing
appearance

of the man at

the door.

Good morning, Mr Strickland, MY name is Mr Daniels,

said Samuel Nathaniel Daniels.

33

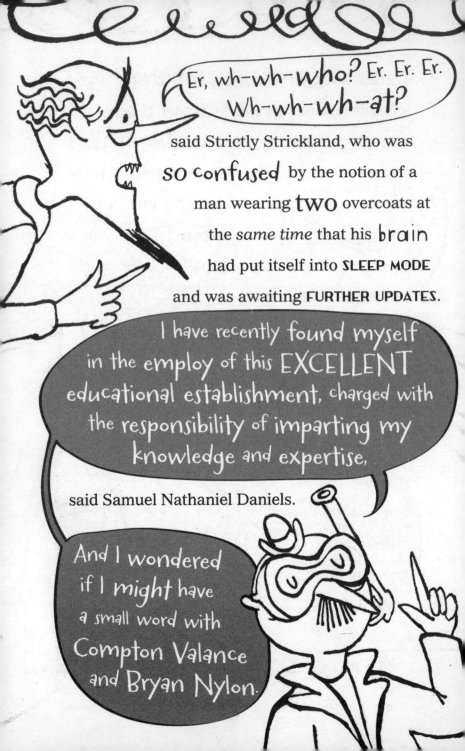

Er, wh-wh-who? Er. Er. Er. Wh-wh-wh-at?

said Strictly Strickland, who was **so confused** by the notion of a man wearing **two** overcoats at the *same time* that his **brain** had put itself into **SLEEP MODE** and was awaiting **FURTHER UPDATES**.

I have recently found myself in the employ of this EXCELLENT educational establishment, charged with the responsibility of imparting my knowledge and expertise,

said Samuel Nathaniel Daniels.

And I wondered if I might have a small word with Compton Valance and Bryan Nylon.

Still struggling with the **StrangeNess** of the situation, Strickland turned to face Compton and performed a *near*-perfect impersonation of a **confused goldfish** by opening and closing his mouth **three times** without making a sound.

???!!!!

Seizing their chance, Compton and Bryan stood up and quickly walked out of the classroom, shutting the door behind them.

It's alright, boys, smiled Samuel Nathaniel Daniels, removing the diving mask and snorkel with a flourish.

It's me! Samuel!

Compton turned to Bryan and raised an eyebrow.

We KNOW!

That is the worst disguise EVER, said Bryan.

Isn't this what ALL teachers wear? said Samuel Nathaniel Daniels.

NO! said Compton.

No teacher has EVER looked like THAT.*

"Are you coming to take us for **PHASE TWO TRAINING**?" said Bryan.

Samuel Nathaniel Daniels looked at his **W.A.T.CH.** and shook his head.

"Don't be silly, **PHASE TWO TRAINING** doesn't start for another four weeks! No, I thought you might like to know what has been going on in the twenty-seventh century since the GRADUATION CEREMONY."**

---

* This is not quite true. A Ms Valerie Colmer once wore a very similar outfit in 1979. She was teaching a series of lessons on Deep Sea Diving in Shallow Waters (When it's Very, Very, Very Cold).

** To put it simply, at the Phase One graduation ceremony, Compton and Bryan stopped Gussage St Vincent from becoming RULER OF THE UNIVERSE. Gussage was being helped by one of his shipmates, called Beverley, and his great, great grandson Scawby Briggs, who was also a student at the F.A.R.T. Academy.

Compton and Bryan's eyes **widened**.

"Oh *yes*," they said, moving a little closer to Samuel Nathaniel Daniels. "What's happened?"

Samuel Nathaniel Daniels looked around to make sure no one was listening and leaned in to Compton and Bryan.

NOTHING really. Everything is pretty much the same as it was. Just thought you'd like to know. See you in a couple of days.

And with that, he pushed some buttons on his **W.A.T.CH.**, the air around him crackled and fizzed and he DISAPPEARED back to the twenty-seventh century.

Compton was about to say something very, **very rude** when the air in the corridor **crackled** and **fizzed** (again) and Samuel Nathaniel Daniels **APPEARED** (again), this time wearing an **ENORMOUS** paper **bag** with a **big hole** cut out for his face.

WHY are you wearing a paper bag?

said Bryan.

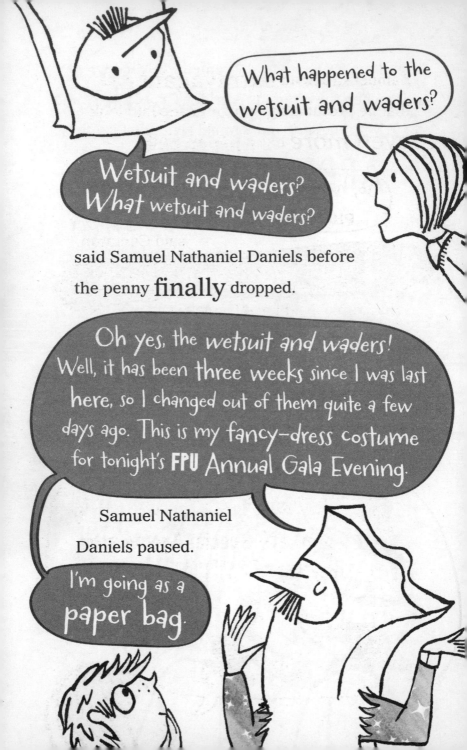

What happened to the wetsuit and waders?

Wetsuit and waders? What wetsuit and waders?

said Samuel Nathaniel Daniels before the penny **finally** dropped.

Oh yes, the *wetsuit and waders!* Well, it has been three weeks since I was last here, so I changed out of them quite a few days ago. This is my fancy–dress costume for tonight's **FPU** Annual Gala Evening.

Samuel Nathaniel Daniels paused.

I'm going as a **paper bag.**

Samuel struck an extravagant pose that he presumably thought made him look even more like a paper bag.

So, have you come to get us for PHASE TWO TRAINING now?

said Compton.

No, it doesn't start for another four days,

said Samuel Nathaniel Daniels.

I've got some news about Beverley and Scawby Briggs for you though.

What happened to them? said Bryan.

The last time we saw them they were being hauled off by some FPU Special Agents after they tried to STEAL our TIME MACHINE SANDWICH.

Well then, you'll be pleased to know that Scawby has been given a **ten-year** sentence in the high-security Time Crim Prison.

"Good riddance," said Bryan. "He'll have a good **long** time to think about what a **horrible bully** he is."

"What about Beverley?" said Compton.

Well because he helped Gussage St Vincent put together the plot to steal the sandwich and ALSO helped Gussage St Vincent kidnap Bryan, he has been given a one-hundred-year sentence.

"A hundred years!" said Bryan. "That is a *really* **long** time."

Yes it is, nodded Samuel Nathaniel Daniels.

It's largely due to Gussage St Vincent getting himself killed and eaten by a sabre-toothed tiger when he used Stinky Trevor to TRAVEL BACK IN TIME twenty thousand years.* You see, Beverley was given the sentence that Gussage *would* have received as well as his own.

* Stinky Trevor is one of the oldest TIME TRAVEL MACHINES **EVER** created. It is kept in **The Time Museum** and can only send the user back to one specific moment in time: 22nd August 17336 BCE. After trying and failing to steal Compton and Bryan's **TIME MACHINE SANDWICH** during a ceremony at **The Time Museum**, Gussage used Stinky Trevor to escape.

43

Compton looked at Bryan.

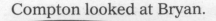

So ALL the bad guys are accounted for and nothing else can *possibly* go wrong,

said Samuel Nathaniel Daniels cheerfully.

Compton was **not at _all_** convinced.

In his recent experience, whenever Samuel

Nathaniel Daniels had used the phrase

"nothing else can *possibly* go wrong",

everything else

had usually gone

MASSIVELY
WRONG

not long after.

"Right then, boys," said Samuel Nathaniel Daniels, pushing some buttons on his **W.A.T.CH.** "I'll be back in four days."

And with **that** the air around him crackled and fizzed (again) and for the second time that day Samuel Nathaniel Daniels DISAPPEARED from the corridor just outside the science room of St Geoffrey's Junior School.

Three seconds later the air in the corridor just outside the science room of St Geoffrey's Junior School crackled and fizzed (again) and Samuel Nathaniel Daniels APPEARED (again).

This time he was wearing the regulation **FPU** tight silver suit and a bowler hat that was at least three sizes too small.

"Okay, boys, are you ready for PHASE TWO TRAINING at the F. A. R. T. Academy?"

Compton and Bryan traded excited looks.

"YES!" they both yelled.

"Alright then, let's go," said Samuel Nathaniel Daniels as he set his W.A.T.CH. to take them to the evening of Sunday, 2nd October 2664, the night before PHASE TWO TRAINING was due to begin. He pushed a button, the air in the corridor crackled and fizzed and they

DISAPPEARED INTO THE FUTURE.

Chapter 4

The GREAT FISH-SLAPPING Game of the Eighteenth Century

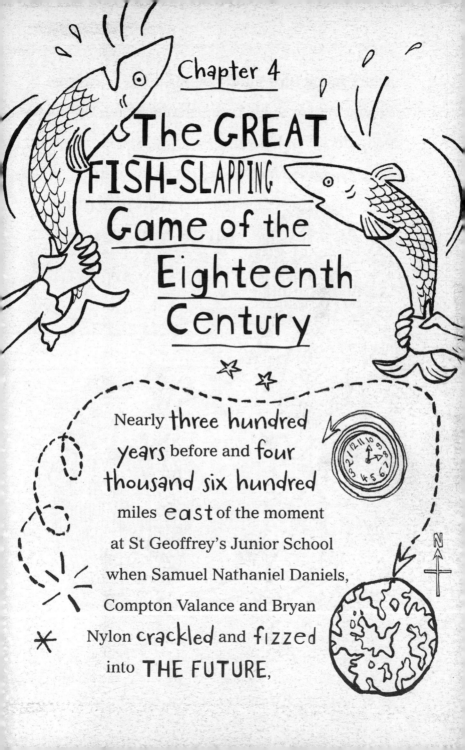

Nearly **three hundred years** before and **four thousand six hundred** miles *east* of the moment at St Geoffrey's Junior School when Samuel Nathaniel Daniels, Compton Valance and Bryan Nylon **crackled** and **fizzed** into **THE FUTURE,**

a very much **alive** and not-at-all eaten Gussage St Vincent sat in his favourite deckchair on the poop deck* of his ship, *Fandango's Revenge*. He looked **glum** as he limply stroked his **ridiculously large moustache**.

> It's, er, your turn, Master.

* Just in case you were wondering, a "poop deck" is a deck that forms the roof of a cabin built at the rear of a ship. It is not the deck where shipmates go to the toilet! (Well, not very often anyway.)

First mate, Jinxy LaBabbage, pointed towards a large barrel of fish.**

Gussage St Vincent sighed.

Not now, Jinxy, I've only just got back from a really, really horrid trip,

he said, fanning himself.

I was very nearly CAPTURED and put in the high-security Time Crim Prison, you know!

** Until quite recently the first mate of *Fandango's Revenge* had been a man called Beverley. Sadly, at this moment he is rather tied up, well locked up, in the high-security Time Crim Prison in the twenty-seventh century.

Jinxy gave the barrel a pat.

Oh, go on, Master, it'll make you feel better.

Gussage sighed again.

Nothing will EVER make me feel better,

he said looking, if anything,

even glummer than before.

I'm trapped, you see, trapped.

Jinxy LaBabbage looked around at the beautiful deep blue waters of the Caribbean Sea.

"Trapped, Master? Out 'ere? Wi' no law or navy for hundreds o' miles?" he said, gesturing towards a flock of large brown pelicans. "No one's trapped out 'ere, Master. Why, we're freer than those swoopin' gango jay birds over yonder."

Gussage St Vincent watched the birds and **sighed** again.

Not ME, I'm afraid, Jinx old bean, he said.

I'm more DOOMED than a banana at a chimp convention. It's only a matter of TIME before the **FPU** discover that I BRILLIANTLY escaped their clutches and, when they *do*, they'll send another team of **Special Agents** back in time to capture me. ALL they need to do is go back to the moment, twenty thousand years ago, that Stinky Trevor sent me to. There's NO WAY I'd be able to avoid them a second time.

They'll arrest me, take me back to that ghastly Time Crim Prison and throw away the key. I CAN'T go back to prison, I'm far too handsome and the clothes they make you wear are HIDEOUS.

Jinxy LaBabbage thought for a moment.

Well, perhaps a small bit of exercise would help get that GREAT BIG noggin' of yours workin' on a solution to your problem,

he said, smiling and stroking the barrel of fish invitingly.

Gussage St Vincent stood up, smoothed down his trousers and walked over to the barrel.

"Oh, *very well*," he said selecting a HUGE fish and yanking it out.

"Perhaps you're right."

"Ah, a tuna, an EXCELLENT choice," said Jinxy LaBabbage, admiring the beautiful silver scales of the four-foot-long fishy MONSTER.

Gussage St Vincent s w i s h e d the GIGANTIC tuna around his head a few times before slinging it over his shoulder.

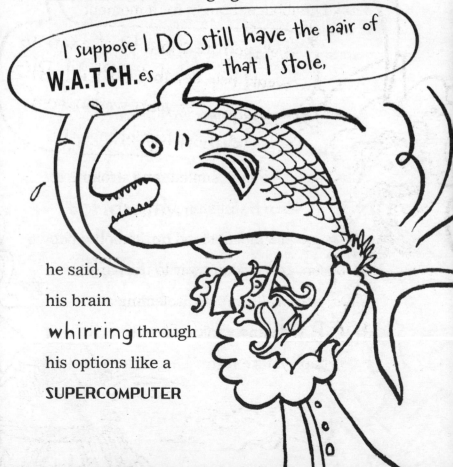

I suppose I DO still have the pair of W.A.T.CH.es that I stole,

he said,

his brain

whirring through

his options like a

SUPERCOMPUTER

as he walked down the stairs of the poop deck and onto the main deck below.

"That you do, sir, that you do," said Jinxy LaBabbage from a few paces behind. "And I'm sure that a quite BRILLIANT plan to save yoursel' from being captured is not very far from revealin' itself to your most wondrous and fabulous self, Master."

Gussage St Vincent stopped at a gap between two cannons.

"Do you really think so?" he said.

"As sure as anything," said Jinxy LaBabbage.

Gussage St Vincent smiled for the first time since he had narrowly avoided being captured by the FPU, stole two of their W.A.T.CH.es and returned from the twenty-seventh century a few days earlier.*

"MEMBERS OF THE FEARLESS," screamed Jinxy LaBabbage. "ASSUME POSITIONS!"**

Still gripping the ENORMOUS fish, Gussage St Vincent felt it wriggle momentarily over his shoulder as he watched the entire despicable crew of *Fandango's Revenge* line up in front of him.

* For a more detailed explanation of EXACTLY how Gussage St Vincent escaped from the FPU please go to the website www.futureperfectunit.com. Basically though, when a Special Agent was sent back to 17336 BCE to arrest him, Gussage simply took advantage of an unfortunate and highly improbable accident with a sabre-toothed tiger, a HUGE rock and an extraordinarily tangled creeper vine. After neutralizing the Special Agent, Gussage stole his identity, fooled the FPU Commissioner and used the Agent's W.A.T.CH. to travel back from 2664 to the year 1732, where he chartered a small boat and sailed back to *Fandango's Revenge* which was moored in its secret hiding place in the Caribbean Sea. You see, his escape was VERY straightforward.

** Gussage St Vincent named his pirate crew The Fearless in 1713. This was partly because it made them sound unbelievably tough and scary and partly because he didn't like their previous name, The Plunderin' Lootin' 'Orrible Pirates, as it was often shortened to The PLOPs.

He s l o w l y walked the length of
The Fearless. First in line and standing
next to the small railing that ran around the edge
of the main deck was Owl-eyed Derek, next to
him was No-pants Terry, then next to him was
Immaculate Kate, next to her was Moon-faced
Neil, next to him was Spectacular Nigel, next
to Spectacular Nigel was Two-planks Mary,
and next to her was Ham-fisted Jack.

Gussage walked past every member of
The Fearless before finally taking his
position in front of Ham-fisted Jack.
He bent down and looked him directly
in the eye, smiling so that his

rows of silver teeth glinted in the early

morning sunlight.

"READY, FEARLESS?" shouted

Jinxy LaBabbage.

"AYE AYE!" shouted back The

Fearless.

Jinxy LaBabbage turned towards Gussage.

ALL IS READY, MASTER, LET THE GAME COMMENCE.

Using both his hands, Gussage St Vincent held the MAGNIFICENT tuna by the tail and got ready to swing. As everyone on board *Fandango's Revenge* held their breath, the only sound that could be heard was the gentle lapping of the Caribbean Sea against the hull of the galleon. The quiet was broken by an *almighty scream* that came out of Gussage's mouth as he swung the HUGE fish with all his might and slapped Ham-fisted Jack on the shoulder with it.

AAARRRRGGGGGHHH!!!

Like an ENORMOUS line of dominoes, each member of the crew fell into the next. Ham-fisted Jack was thrown sideways into Two-planks Mary, who in turn bashed into Spectacular Nigel, who then (bumped) into Moon-faced Neil, who ≩CRASHED≩ against Immaculate Kate, who slammed into No-pants Terry, who shunted into Owl-eyed Derek, who, having no one next to him to bump into, fell head first into the sea below.

He tossed the rather shell-shocked tuna into the sea. It bounced off Owl-eyed Derek's face and swam away in disgust. As the fish DISAPPEARED into the distance and Gussage looked at the horizon beyond, an idea of OUTRAGEOUS proportions hit him full in the brain like a runaway fridge. An idea so devious that he wouldn't just save himself from the hideous prospect of being captured and thrown in prison, but would also fulfil his dream of

ENSLAVING HUMANITY

and becoming

THE MASTER OF TIME.

FETCH ME MY FINEST TRAVELLING TROUSERS IMMEDIATELY!

he roared.

I need to go back to the twenty-seventh century, just before the moment that I escape from the **FPU** by using Stinky Trevor to travel back twenty-thousand years.

"What will you do **there**, Master?" said Jinxy LaBabbage.

"Well," said Gussage. "I'll tell myself **NOT** to use Stinky Trevor to travel back twenty-thousand years. If I escape in a **different** way, then the **FPU** won't be able to capture me twenty-thousand years ago!"

Jinxy La Babbage stared blankly as Gussage strode off towards his cabin.

Sometimes I 'ave absolutely NO idea what he's on about,

Jinxy said as he went to fetch Gussage's brand-new green-and-white striped TRAVELLING TROUSERS.*

* Gussage St Vincent felt that EVERY pirate worth his salt should have a pair of trousers for EVERY occasion. Gussage himself had trousers for travelling, thinking, walking, playing backgammon, eating, sitting on the toilet, snoozing (morning), reading, marauding, snoozing (afternoon) and SHOUTING.

Chapter 5

2nd October 2684, 6.30 p.m.

No one quite knows the **exact** reason why Samuel Nathaniel Daniels's **W.A.T.CH.** took him, Compton and Bryan to the year **2684** rather than **266̲4**. To be perfectly honest with you it was probably because Samuel Nathaniel Daniels had **NOT** been paying attention and had accidentally pushed the wrong button or something. *

* In Samuel Nathaniel Daniels's life as an **FPU** agent, he had accidentally pushed the wrong button on his W.A.T.CH. no fewer than eighty-four times. The most embarrassing moment had been when, instead of travelling to the year 2013, he had *actually* travelled BACK to the year 1013 and caught the great Viking King, Sweyn Forkbeard, using a leaf to wipe his bottom.

In the end though, the reason WHY it had happened didn't matter nearly as much as the fact that it HAD happened. You see, in the school classrooms of the centuries to come, what Samuel Nathaniel Daniels, Compton and Bryan were about to find out would be seen as one of the MOST IMPORTANT DISCOVERIES IN THE WHOLE HISTORY OF THE UNIVERSE.

As the air around them crackled and fizzed, Compton immediately realized that something in the twenty-seventh century was very, very WRONG.

They had arrived exactly where they wanted to be, slap-bang in the middle of the FPU Arrivals Hall, it just wasn't the FPU Arrivals Hall that any of them remembered, or expected.

The beginning of a new term of
training should have meant that the
place was {buzzing} with activity.
Academy Agents *should*
have been crackling and
fizzing onto the specially
marked arrival zones...

excited chatter should
have been echoing
around the hall...

and **FPU** Agents should have been
holding glistening bogeys
for **REGISTRATION** purposes. *

* The **Future Perfect Unit** developed a security system
based on an individual's snot pattern. Called BRT, or
BOGEY RECOGNITION TECHNOLOGY, it relies on a
database that has all Academy Agents and **FPU** workers'
DNA on it. This is then cross-referenced with the DNA
in someone's nasal mucus to confirm their identity.

What Compton and Bryan actually saw as they looked around, was the Arrivals Hall in ruins. The walls were cracked and crumbling, the once sparkling registration desks were now battered and shabby and the

WHOLE HUGE SPACE WAS

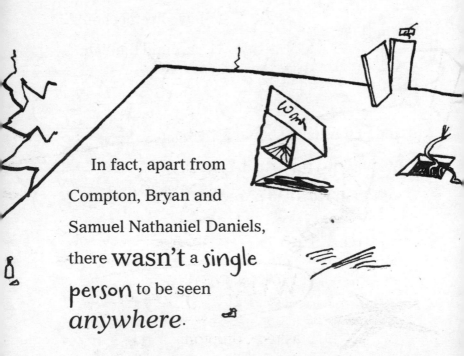

In fact, apart from Compton, Bryan and Samuel Nathaniel Daniels, there wasn't a single person to be seen anywhere.

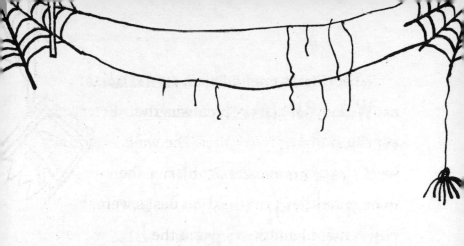

EERILY EMPTY.

WHAT'S going on?

asked Compton.

Samuel Nathaniel Daniels hit the side of his **W.A.T.CH. hard**, causing it to beep angrily at him.

"I don't understand," he said, continuing to push buttons furiously. "We are in the right place on the right day but we're in COMPLETELY the wrong year. It's 6.30 p.m. on the second of October, the day before the beginning of term, but we've come to 2684, not 2664."

"2684," said Bryan. "So we're twenty years ahead of where we should be?"

"Yes, but something has gone very, very WRONG," said Samuel Nathaniel Daniels, hitting his **W.A.T.CH.** again.

The place is in RUINS. I DON'T like this one little bit.

Compton looked around the strange Arrivals Hall. Every so often HOLOGRAPHIC POSTERS would APPEAR.

"Oh my," he said, nudging Bryan and pointing to one that had APPEARED on the other side of the hall. "Look!"

It took a moment for Bryan to see what Compton was pointing at.

Baked bean sale at Mad Kev's?

he read slowly.

"Crazy knockdown prices? Everything must go?" *

Compton sighed.

"Well I see that that **does** represent **extraordinarily** good value for money," continued Bryan. "**But** shouldn't we be concentrating on **WHY** the **FUTURE** is all **tatty** and in **ruins**?"

"Not **THAT** poster," said Compton. "The one *next* to it."

He pointed to the words, which read:

"Oh **yes**," said Bryan. "I see."

* Baked beans still exist in the twenty-seventh century but are mainly used for cleaning toilets.

A tinny bugle fanfare started to play as a
HUGE HOLOGRAPHIC HEAD
APPEARED
out of nowhere and hovered above them.

GOOD
MORNING,
SUBJECTS,

said the

HOLOGRAPHIC
HEAD.

Gussage St Vincent!

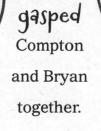

gasped
Compton
and Bryan
together.

73

I AM PLEASED TO ANNOUNCE THAT, AS <u>TODAY</u> IS MY BIRTHDAY, I SHALL BE GIVING YOU ALL A *VERY SPECIAL* TREAT. IN HONOUR OF ME, GUSSAGE ST VINCENT, YOUR OVERLORD AND MASTER, EVERYONE IS GIVEN THE AFTERNOON OFF TO ASSEMBLE AT THE GUSSAGE DOME ON GUSSAGE AVENUE IN THE ST VINCENT 1 DISTRICT. PLEASE PLACE YOUR GIFTS AND TRIBUTES TO ME THERE, WHERE I SHALL PICK THEM ALL UP LATER. <u>DO NOT</u> FORGET BECAUSE I'LL BE WATCHING <u>*ALL OF YOU.*</u>

Then, just as quickly as it had appeared, the HOLOGRAPHIC HEAD of Gussage St Vincent VANISHED.

"Er, I *thought* he had been killed and eaten by a sabre-toothed tiger twenty thousand years ago," said Bryan.

Samuel Nathaniel Daniels gulped and furiously hit some buttons on his W.A.T.CH. The air in the Arrivals Hall crackled and fizzed and he, Compton and Bryan DISAPPEARED INTO THE PAST.

Chapter 6

Nineteen Years, Three Hundred and Sixty-Four Days Earlier

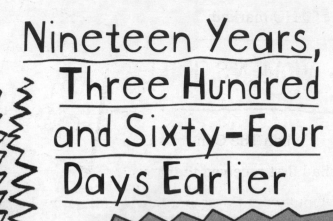

GUSSAGE ST WHAT MUST STILL BE _WHAT_?

yelled The Commissioner

as she sat behind

the desk

in her

super-secret

office,

which was hidden behind a door in the
FPU HQ marked

WOMEN'S TOILETS

OUT OF ORDER*.

When The Commissioner
had first received the news
about what Compton, Bryan and Samuel
Nathaniel Daniels had seen in the year 2684,
the shock had been so GREAT that she had
actually yelled, "WHAT WHAT WHAT
WHAT WHAT WHAT _WHAT_?"
Now, with each passing moment her
astonishment was slowly
receding and the power of
language was
returning.

* As a cunning security device,
some of the twenty-seventh century's
MOST secret rooms are hidden behind
doors with strange signs on them.

In another couple of **minutes**, The Commissioner would be able to complete the sentence, "Gussage St Vincent **must** still be *ALIVE*?"

It's the ONLY explanation,

said Samuel Nathaniel Daniels.

But thanks to Compton and Bryan, we closed this case **three months ago**,

said The Commissioner.

We had Gussage St Vincent cornered when he went back in time EXACTLY twenty-thousand years and I sent a **Special Agent** back to capture him. He ASSURED me that he had seen Gussage St Vincent attacked and eaten by a sabre-toothed tiger.

Samuel Nathaniel Daniels took off his tiny bowler hat and **scratched** his head. This was something he often did in moments of **EXTREME** stress.

Er, well, er, Commissioner, it would appear, er, that the, er, **Special Agent** who **ASSURED** you about Gussage,

he said, **anxiously** running his fingers around the brim of his hat,

WAS, in fact, er, Gussage St Vincent HIMSELF.

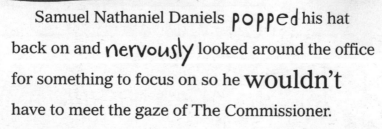

Samuel Nathaniel Daniels **popped** his hat back on and **nervously** looked around the office for something to focus on so he **wouldn't** have to meet the gaze of The Commissioner.

He settled on watching the

HOLOGRAPHIC PROJECTION

of the news programme that The Commissioner

always had on in the corner of her office

with the sound turned down.

If there is ONE thing that I really hate,

said The Commissioner, as she
stopped rubbing her temples
and began cracking her knuckles,

it is a case that I thought was closed SUDDENLY opening up again!

Compton looked at Bryan and then back

at The Commissioner.

Isn't it OBVIOUS what we've GOT to do?

he said.

We've GOT to go and get him! I mean, EVEN if Gussage wasn't eaten by a sabre-toothed tiger twenty thousand years ago, you still know that's WHERE he went. So WHY don't you just send a team of agents BACK to a few minutes <u>before</u> THAT moment where they can wait for him to APPEAR and then they can arrest him WHEN he APPEARS.

The Commissioner stopped cracking her knuckles and stood up from her chair.

You mean engage a **PROTOCOL 4 TIME CRIM ARREST SEQUENCE?**

she said and began pacing the floor of her office.

Well, it could work, I suppose. What do YOU think, Agent Daniels?

Samuel Nathaniel Daniels paused for a moment. "Well, as long as Gussage *hasn't* worked out how to complete a **SECTION 9** then I *think* it's a *good* idea," he said.

"Yes, a **SECTION 9** of a **PROTOCOL 4 TCAS** worries **me** too," said The Commissioner.

Bryan looked at Compton.

"What are they talking about?" he whispered.

Compton shrugged his shoulders.

"Still, it's worth a *go*," said The Commissioner. "But for a job like *this* we need the **BEST TIME CRIM TRACKER** the **FPU** has **EVER** known."

You DON'T mean...?

Yes, I most positively DO mean,

said The Commissioner.

Get me LANGLEY VON TINKLEHORN!

Langley Von Tinklehorn?

Langley Von Tinklehorn.

THE Langley Von Tinklehorn?

THE Langley. Von. TINKLEHORN.

Compton looked at Bryan.

"Who's Langley Von Tinklehorn?" he said.

ME, said a DEEP, gravelly, heroic-sounding voice from the shadows at the back of The Commissioner's office.

I'M LANGLEY VON TINKLEHORN!

Chapter 7

LANGLEY VON TINKLEHORN

The mouths of Compton Valance, Bryan Nylon, Samuel Nathaniel Daniels and The Commissioner hit the **floor**. They couldn't help but **goggle** at the **fabulous** and **HEROIC** **dash** that Langley Von Tinklehorn cut as he emerged **mysteriously** from the shadows.

He was **tall**, dressed in a **long** black, hooded leather coat and **black** trousers, covered with mirrored stars.

"An **ABSOLUTE** legend," whispered back Samuel Nathaniel Daniels. "He's the **FPU** Agent who has captured **more Time Crims** than **anyone** else. He retired over **fifteen years ago** but **EVERYONE** has heard the stories about him. How he **captured** Telford Madeley *single-handed* back in **'39** and **cracked** the notorious Kettering case in **'47**."

L-L-Langley? stammered The Commissioner, who was clearly in a state of **SHOCK** at Langley Von Tinklehorn's **sudden** and **exceptionally dramatic** entrance.

B-but. W-why? I-I-mean, h-h-how?

Von Tinklehorn held up his hand and
The Commissioner fell silent.

Don't worry, I'm TOTALLY up to speed,

he said, immediately adopting a
classic **Action Hero #4 pose**,
as detailed on page twenty-four
of the

OFFICIAL EARTH 1 HERO ASSOCIATION'S REGULATION HANDBOOK.*

* The official EARTH 1 HERO ASSOCIATION'S REGULATION HANDBOOK was a publishing sensation in 2650. It lists EVERY known heroic pose for EVERY known heroic occasion.

You need me to go **BACK IN TIME** twenty thousand years, engage a **PROTOCOL 4 TIME CRIM ARREST SEQUENCE** and apprehend Gussage St Vincent?

The Commissioner regained her composure and ran a hand through her **long** wavy hair.

That's **RIGHT**,

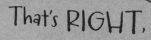

she said.

But we're worried that he might pull off a **SECTION 9**. Do you need back up?

Langley Von Tinklehorn shook his head and smiled.

And with **that** he pushed a
button on his **W.A.T.CH.** and
DISAPPEARED.

"What's a **SECTION 9**?" said Compton eventually.

Still looking at the space where Langley had just DISAPPEARED, The Commissioner shook her head and turned to Compton and Bryan.

"Well, Langley has gone BACK twenty thousand years to the spot that Gussage St Vincent travelled to, *right?*"

"Right!" said Compton and Bryan.

And we're ASSUMING that this TIMELINE is going to work out EXACTLY as it did before, right?

Right!

said Compton and Bryan.

"So, *if* it **does**, then Gussage will **materialize** at the **same** spot and at **EXACTLY** the **same** time, **twenty thousand years ago**, that he did before. Only *this time* Langley Von Tinklehorn, the **GREATEST TIME CRIM TRACKER THE WORLD HAS EVER KNOWN** will be waiting to **arrest** him."

"**Brilliant**," said Compton.

"**PERFECT**," said Bryan.

"Ah *yes*, but *what if* the Gussage that escaped from here first time round works out that we would **obviously** think of setting a **trap** to capture him and so goes back to a **moment** *before* he travels back in time to **warn himself** to escape some **other** way – a way **we** don't know about? In that new **TIMELINE**, he *won't* travel back **twenty thousand years** and Langley *won't* capture him. That's a ***SECTION 9***."

"Oh," said Compton.

Just then the air in The Commissioner's office **crackled** and **fizzed**

and Langley Von Tinklehorn

REAPPEARED.

He DIDN'T show up,

he said, assuming the near impossible *FLYING BADGER* Pose.

It was a textbook *SECTION 9*!

Everyone **immediately** covered
their **noses** with their hands.

"**What** on earth is that **TERRIBLE**
smell?" said The Commissioner, looking
around her office.

"**Ah**, I'm afraid that's **me**," said Langley,
looking down at his dirty, thigh-high black
boots. "I **materialized** right in the middle of an
ENORMOUS PILE of **POO**."

Urgh! said Bryan,
holding his nose.

That is a *really* horrible
STINK. It doesn't smell like
ANYTHING I've
ever stepped in.

Langley removed his boot and, eyeing the gunk on the bottom of it, held it up to his nose. He took a

HUGE
sniff

and then grabbed a GREAT glob of the gunk and rubbed it between his thumb and forefinger.

My guess is sabre-toothed tiger,

he said.

Female. Young. And has recently EATEN something that disagreed with her.

"I tell you **what**, Langley,"
said The Commissioner,
her hand still **clamped**
hard on her nose.
"You **pop** and change
your **shoes**.
We won't do
anything
until you're back."

Right!

said Langley, briefly
adopting the **VERTICAL
SHARK Pose** before he
pushed some buttons
on his **W.A.T.CH.** and
DISAPPEARED
from the office.

Chapter 8

Another EXTRAORDINARY Entrance

The atmosphere in The Commissioner's super-secret office was SO TENSE it could have been a sequel to the movie,

TENSE OFFICE,

called

TENSE OFFICE 2:
THE TENSION RISES.

Compton, Bryan, Samuel Nathaniel Daniels and Langley Von Tinklehorn (freshly booted) all stood and watched as The Commissioner paced the floor.*

SO, to recap, said The Commissioner.

Gussage St Vincent, the most DANGEROUS TIME CRIM in HISTORY and a man who, up until a few minutes ago, we thought was DEAD, is actually very much ALIVE.

* Well, Compton, Bryan and Samuel Nathaniel Daniels all stood. Langley Von Tinklehorn had adopted a highly complicated pose called THE ELEVATED GRAVY BOAT.

"Yes," said Samuel Nathaniel Daniels.

Not only THAT, said The Commissioner, but we have absolutely NO IDEA where or when in the world he IS because he has somehow managed to get his hands on a W.A.T.CH.

"That's right," said Samuel Nathaniel Daniels.

All we KNOW is that in some version of THE FUTURE, twenty years from NOW, he is GUSSAGE ST VINCENT, OVERLORD OF THE UNIVERSE.

"Yes," said Samuel Nathaniel Daniels. The Commissioner **stopped pacing** and turned to look out of her ENORMOUS window.

There's only ONE THING for it,

she said to **no one** in particular before dialling a number on her **HandPhone.** *

---

* In the twenty-seventh century, the HANDPHONE allows you to dial a number on the palm of your hand. Then you put your thumb in your ear and speak into your little finger. In fact, it's just like the way twenty-first century people make the "I'll call you" sign with their hand.

99

Compton glanced at Langley Von Tinklehorn, who had started to

s l o w l y spin around... through ALL eight... BRAZILIAN WHIPLASH poses.

GET ME THE HUSH-HUSH TOP SECRET OPERATIONS ROOM,

she **barked** at whoever was on the other end of the line.

We've got an EMERGENCY SITUATION and I need as many **FPU** agents as possible to run through possible FUTURE TIMELINES. And I NEED this to happen YESTERDAY!

The Commissioner pushed the palm of her hand and the call ended.

"Right, HERE'S what we're going to do," she said to everyone. "We have to make sure that THE FUTURE that you saw in twenty years' time NEVER comes true."

Compton, Bryan, Samuel Nathaniel Daniels and Langley Von Tinklehorn all nodded.

To do that, Samuel Nathaniel Daniels and I are going to take charge of the HUSH-HUSH TOP SECRET OPERATIONS ROOM. We'll run through as many possible TIMELINES as we can. Who knows, we might get LUCKY and stumble on the ONE that creates THE FUTURE that you saw. If we do, then we'll know EXACTLY what Gussage's plan IS and HOW it will play out.

And if we know THAT,

said Samuel Nathaniel Daniels,

then we'll know WHEN and WHERE he will turn up and then we can ARREST him.

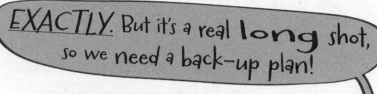

EXACTLY. But it's a real **long** shot, so we need a back-up plan!

said The Commissioner and she turned to face Langley Von Tinklehorn.

Langley, you're the <u>BEST</u> TIME CRIM TRACKER there IS. I need you to go through Gussage St Vincent's history. We might be able to find out WHAT he's after from something that we already know about him. I want NO stone left unturned.

Langley thought for a **moment** using the

Dropped Knee Contemplation Pose.

"It'll be quicker if I have some help,"

he said eventually.

The Commissioner turned to face Compton
and Bryan.

"How about it, boys?" she said.

"It has been

three months

since you last

SAVED

THE

UNIVERSE."

Compton and Bryan

smiled at each other

and high-fived.

"We're IN!" said Compton.

"EXCELLENT," smiled The Commissioner.

Just imagine it. The WORLD FAMOUS Compton Valance and Bryan Nylon team up with the GREATEST Time Crim Tracker EVER. It's SENSATIONAL!

"You *could* call yourself the Little Tinkles," said Langley Von Tinklehorn.

Compton and Bryan immediately stopped smiling.

"Er, maybe not," said Bryan.

"Well, we can iron out those details later," said The Commissioner. "The **important** thing is that we **know** Gussage St Vincent is in possession of at *least* one **W.A.T.CH.** From what we already know about **THE FUTURE**, and based on St Vincent's track record, every **instinct** in my body tells me that he'll be using his **mad evil GENIUS** to create a **bigger** and **better TIME MACHINE** than just one or two **W.A.T.CH.**es."

"Could he still turn his pirate ship into a **TIME MACHINE**?" asked Compton. "Like he was going to do last time?"

The Commissioner thought for a while. "**Hmm**, yes, but he **needed** your **TIME-MACHINE SANDWICH** to **power** it," she said, as Langley Von Tinklehorn adopted the wide-legged *MONGOLIAN SCRATCHING* Pose.

"As he **doesn't** have the sandwich, because it's safely locked away in a top secret location, then I don't see how he could create a TIME MACHINE out of *Fandango's Rev—*"

The Commissioner's answer was cut short as the walls of her office suddenly started to *shake violently* and a **deafening scraping** sound filled the air.

WHAT'S GOING ON?

shouted Samuel Nathaniel Daniels as he struggled to remain on his feet.

The Commissioner **staggered** towards her ENORMOUS seventy-second-floor window and looked out. Whatever was making the noise was *so* close to the **FPU** HQ building that it kept bumping and scraping across her office windowpane.

The Commissioner punched a number into her **HandPhone**.

"Surveillance, are you seeing *this*?" she **barked**. "I want all eyes on it *NOW!*"

"WHAT IS *THAT?* IT'S MASSIVE!" yelled Compton.

As the ENORMOUS object eventually moved past the window, Compton's question was answered.

He watched, open-mouthed, at the sight of a **HUGE**, flying pirate galleon bearing the name *Fandango's Revenge* on its side. Worst of **all**, standing right there on deck, his **IMMENSE** moustache flapping in the wind, was the **MOST DASTARDLY TIME CRIM IN HISTORY** and a man who, up until a few minutes earlier, the **whole world** had thought was **DEAD...**

GUSSAGE ST VINCENT! yelled

The Commissioner.

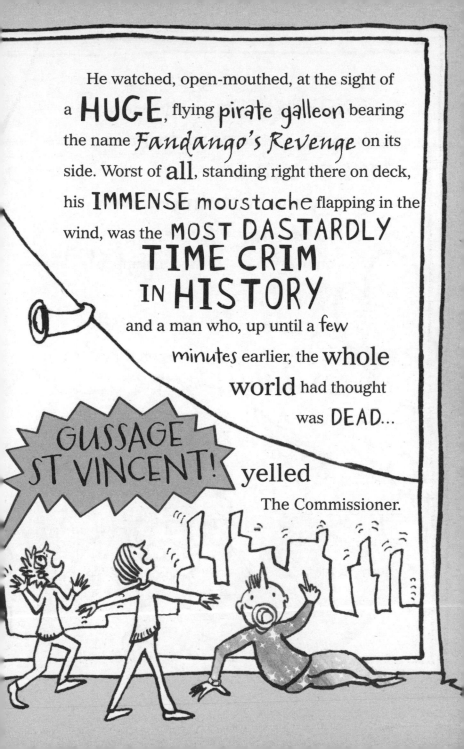

"Can't someone use their **W.A.T.CH.** to transport themselves onto the ship and GRAB him?" said Compton, turning round and looking at The Commissioner.

They all watched as Gussage yelled at Jinxy LaBabbage while the rest of The Fearless crew struggled to hold on to the side of the ship.

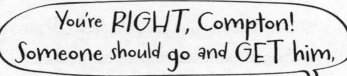

You're RIGHT, Compton! Someone should go and GET him,

Langley said. And THAT person is ME!

And with that, Langley Von Tinklehorn briefly adopted the ceremonial **ECUADORIAN ACTION STATIONS** Pose before he pushed a few buttons on his **W.A.T.CH.** and

DISAPPEARED.

"Where has he GONE?" said Compton.

As they all watched, the air around *Fandango's Revenge* crackled and fizzed, the galleon spun round and round and *round* about ten times and then DISAPPEARED.

An alarm  bleeped on The Commissioner's **HandPhone**.

"Hello?" she said. "Yes? Yes? I see."

The Commissioner pushed a button and ended the call.

That was the TIME CRIM PRISON,

she said.

There's been a BREAKOUT.

Chapter 9

The Worst-sounding Movie in HISTORY

Compton **whirled** away from the window, **grabbed** a remote control and **turned up** the volume of the HOLOGRAPHIC **news** programme that was silently playing in the corner of The Commissioner's office.

Hi, I'm TED STOAT,

shouted a newsreader sitting behind a desk

emblazoned with the words

NEW NEW NEW LONDON NEWS... NOW!*

Today's BIG NEWS STORY in New New London is the sighting of a MYSTERIOUS UNIDENTIFIED FLYING OBJECT over the **FPU** HQ. Let's go LIVE to our on-the-spot reporter Lenny Cubbage for the LATEST UPDATE.

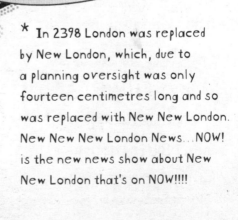

* In 2398 London was replaced by New London, which, due to a planning oversight was only fourteen centimetres long and so was replaced with New New London. New New New London News...NOW! is the new news show about New New London that's on NOW!!!!

"LOOK!" shouted Bryan as he looked out of The Commissioner's window.

I can see the news camera down on the street. COO-EEE! Hello! Lenny! *Up here!*

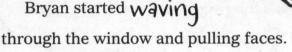

Bryan started waving through the window and pulling faces.

"They won't be able to see you," said Samuel Nathaniel Daniels. "Because firstly, the windows have a special coating on them. From the outside it looks like there's a *really* BORING meeting taking place. It's a security device. And secondly, we're seventy-two floors up."

Disappointed, Bryan turned back and watched the news.

"The BIG STORY here," continued Lenny Cubbage, "is that the MYSTERIOUS FLYING OBJECT has just been **IDENTIFIED**. A few moments ago, downtown **New New London** was the scene of a truly **EXTRAORDINARY** sight. A **HUGE** floating PIRATE SHIP materialized out of thin air, hovered above the BUILDING to the left of the **FPU** HQ..."

"That's the secret high-security Time Crim Prison," said The Commissioner.

"...before floating off again, seemingly OUT OF CONTROL, *nearly* CRASHING into the **FPU** HQ building and then FINALLY DISAPPEARING into thin air."

Lenny Cubbage turned to a **nervy** looking **man** next to him.

Sir, can you tell us what you saw?

Well, it ALL happened so fast,

the **nervy man** began.

But basically, a HUGE floating PIRATE SHIP materialized out of thin air, hovered above the building to the left of the **FPU** HQ, before taking off again, seemingly out of control, nearly CRASHING into the **FPU** HQ building and then DISAPPEARING into thin air.

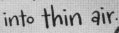

The Commissioner cracked her knuckles.

"Unless we contain this, people are going to start to ⋝panic,⋜" she said. "A pirate ship shouldn't just materialize and float over a major city."

"Why don't you phone into the show?" said Compton. "You don't have to say what really happened, just make something up."

The Commissioner dialled a number on her **HandPhone**.

PUT ME THROUGH TO TED STOAT!

she yelled.

Yes of COURSE I know he's on the air. It's The Commissioner of the **FPU** speaking.

On the HOLOGRAPHIC screen, Ted Stoat **suddenly** put his finger in his ear, like he was being told something, and a picture of The Commissioner flashed up next to him.

On the line, LIVE from the FPU, is The Commissioner,

he said importantly.

Commissioner, you've seen the FOOTAGE. Can you tell us WHAT is GOING ON?

HELLO, Ted,

said The Commissioner in a calm, confident voice.

And can I begin by saying that I REALLY LOVE your show.

Ted Stoat smiled.

I got in touch to reassure your viewers,

The Commissioner continued.

I'm AWARE that a number of people in New New London spotted a floating pirate ship earlier.

That's right, said Ted Stoat.

Well, there's a perfectly simple AND quite innocent explanation for WHAT they saw,

said The Commissioner.

Yes? said Ted Stoat.

And WHAT is the explanation?

The Commissioner looked round at the others and Compton *thought* he saw a single bead of sweat trickle down her face. It was painfully obvious that she had absolutely no idea what to say next.

Er, well,

said The Commissioner stalling for time as she racked her brains for an answer.

Yes?

Er, the pirate ship was...

YES?

"Tell him it was a scene for a new movie that is just being filmed," whispered Compton.

Er, ACTUALLY the pirate ship was, in fact, part of a scene for a new movie that is just being filmed,

repeated The Commissioner.

"A *MOVIE*?" said Ted Stoat in a tone of voice that made Compton think he wasn't **at all** convinced.

"That's right," said The Commissioner.

"What's the MOVIE called?" said Ted Stoat.

Compton quickly turned to Bryan.

"We need to think of a name that sounds like it would have a scene with a flying pirate ship," he said.

THE DOLL'S HOUSE!!

yelled The Commissioner suddenly, in PANIC.

"*THE DOLL'S HOUSE?*" said Ted Stoat.

The Doll's House?

said Compton and Bryan together.

"YES, The Doll's House," repeated The Commissioner.

"And IN a film called THE DOLL'S HOUSE there's a scene that needs a *FLYING PIRATE SHIP?*" said Ted Stoat.

"That's right," said The Commissioner. "When you see it, it will all make PERFECT sense. You'll *love it.* Bye."

And with that The Commissioner pushed a button on her palm and ENDED the call. She pulled out a hanky and dabbed the perspiration from her face.

"*The Doll's House?*" said Compton.

"Seriously, *THAT* was the best you could think of?"

"I was under pressure," she said,

turning the sound down on
NEW NEW NEW
LONDON NEWS... NOW!

"Agent Daniels," she said. "I need you to go now and hire a movie director."

"Er, okay," said Samuel Nathaniel Daniels.

"Then the director has to make a movie called The Doll's House."

"Er, okay," said Samuel Nathaniel Daniels again.

And it most DEFINITELY has to have a scene with a flying pirate ship over New New London.

Er, okay,

repeated Samuel Nathaniel Daniels.

"And then we'll meet back at the HUSH-HUSH TOP SECRET OPERATIONS ROOM in one hour," said The Commissioner.

"Eh?" said Samuel Nathaniel Daniels, only half listening. His brain had started to mull over the possibility of hiring his favourite actress, Angel Delice, for the lead role in The Doll's House.

The Dollshouse

Starring Angel Delice

"The HUSH-HUSH TOP SECRET OPERATIONS ROOM," she repeated. "Where you and I are going to head up the search through possible FUTURE TIMELINES to try and find out what Gussage St Vincent is up to."

"Oh yes, of course," said Samuel Nathaniel Daniels, suddenly remembering the whole WORST-TIME-CRIM-IN-HISTORY-ON-THE-RAMPAGE-THROUGH-TIME SITUATION.

"Well?" said The Commissioner. "What are you waiting for?"

Looking a bit flustered at the thought of having to produce his first movie, Samuel Nathaniel Daniels pushed a button on his W.A.T.CH. and

DISAPPEARED.

"At least now people won't panic about seeing a flying pirate ship," said The Commissioner. "And it should STOP any awkward questions about a break out at the secret high-security TIME CRIM PRISON."

"They must have got in from the roof when the ship landed there," said Compton.

"Yes," sighed The Commissioner as she checked her InfoTab.* "Eight minutes and thirty seconds ago, thanks to Gussage St Vincent somehow making a TIME-TRAVELLING PIRATE SHIP.

* Information Tablet. EVERY FPU agent has their own InfoTab, which is a bit like a hand-held computer.

And, just before it almost crashed into **FPU** HQ, Scawby Briggs escaped from his cell."

"What about Beverley?" said Bryan.

The Commissioner shook her head.

"No, Beverley is still locked up safe and sound," she said. "The reports suggest that the ship moved off again before they had a chance to get him."

Compton scratched his head.

That's *weird.* IF Gussage has built his **TIME-MACHINE PIRATE SHIP** then **WHAT** went **WRONG?** **WHY** did it seem so **out of control?** **WHY** leave before they got Beverley?

A moment later there was a knock at the door of The Commissioner's super-secret office.

The Commissioner opened the door and was handed an **old brown envelope**.

She RIPPED it open.

It's from Langley, she said.

He's STUCK in the eighteenth century.

Chapter 10

The EXTRAORDINARY and DRAMATIC RETURN of

Fandango's Revenge

Miguel Vazquez had been fishing the same waters for the last thirty years but had NEVER known a more disappointing morning than this one. The muscles in his tanned, tattooed arms burned with effort as he rowed his small boat to a better position on the other side of the headland.

Once he was happy, he stopped and glugged deeply from his ENORMOUS bottle of grog.

He was SURE that this bit of sea would yield a more successful afternoon, so after quenching his thirst, he hauled in his oars, cast his net overboard and fell into his usual, DEEP lunchtime snooze.

At exactly 12.14 p.m. on the afternoon of Tuesday 8th August, 1732, the air above the sea just off the coast of the tiny Caribbean island of Iles des Saintes began to crackle and fizz.

At the same time, the sea near Miguel's boat whipped round and round and round, forming itself into a GIANT waterspout. Had Miguel been awake he would have seen a HUGE pirate galleon APPEAR out of THIN AIR about thirty metres above the sea, spinning faster than a ballerina in a washing machine.

zzz....

After twirling furiously, the ship suddenly stopped DEAD and hovered in the air for a moment before plummeting to the sea. The splashdown was SPECTACULAR and ferocious. A HUGE WALL of water was thrown high into the air, spraying the surrounding sea with fish...and sand and seaweed.

Miguel woke to discover his boat half full of water, a small hammerhead shark on his lap and an octopus on his head. Screaming loudly,

AAARRRR-GGGHH!!!

he threw the octopus back in the sea, jumped overboard and swam for shore as quickly as he could. Onboard Fandango's Revenge, the scene was not a pretty one. Members of The Fearless were wobbling around the main deck moaning loudly or being sick over the side.

Hidden in the shadows, behind six

large~stinky~barrels with

MUCKSLOWE MURPHY'S
Caskets o'Fun*

written in them, Langley Von Tinklehorn

picked himself up off the floor and quickly

assumed the **STEALTHY OBSERVING**

Pose. No one seemed to have spotted him

and so, from his secret location, he scanned

the decks and quietly watched the

commotion.

* The contents of a barrel of
Muckslowe Murphy's Caskets o'Fun
were actually about as much fun
as dropping an angry shark down
your pants. Each barrel contained
sheep brains, goat intestines, emu
gizzards, pig entrails and duck giblets
all packed in salt. It was a kind of
lucky-dip of meat to make cooking
onboard ships more exciting.

"W-w-WHA' in the name of Queen Isabella's jewelled natterjacks just 'appened?" murmured Jinxy LaBabbage as he staggered to his feet.

"WHAT just happened," said Gussage St Vincent as he stared out across the beautiful waters of the Caribbean Sea*, "is that I CREATED a temporary power supply, using a single W.A.T.CH., STRONG enough to send an eighteenth-century galleon forward in TIME by nearly a thousand years."

* Due to an accident he'd had with a watering can and a packet of instant noodles when he was four, Gussage St Vincent had NEVER, EVER felt the effects of motion sickness. This meant he was perfectly suited to a life on the high seas, as no matter how rough the crossing, he had NEVER been seasick.

Jinxy **knew** that his master and his former first mate **Beverley** had been through many **adventures** together. Only a man with a truly **black heart** would *not* feel saddened by his absence.

Ah well, can't be helped, can't be helped, said Gussage, rubbing his moustache.

To be honest, I NEVER REALLY liked him anyway. I ALWAYS thought he was a bit of a THUNDERING, BRAINLESS, DUMPLING-FED FUSTINUTS.*

* In the TOP TWENTY list of insults that an eighteenth-century pirate could hurl, the phrase "thundering, brainless, dumpling-fed fustinuts" came in at number fourteen. It was a little bit better than calling someone a "gut-gounding gustifuts" and a bit worse than calling someone a "jaw-me-down Bob Adams". However, if you're ever in the eighteenth century and you *REALLY* want to hurt someone's feelings, then the number one insult to use is ~~jolly-me-twice-slopping-gugar-blubbin~~.

While Jinxy LaBabbage goggled at how disposable his master seemed to find his first mates, Langley plotted his next move from the shadows at the side of the ship. He knew that if he was going to arrest Gussage then he would have to do it soon. The Fearless crew were in a shambolic state after their trip to the twenty-seventh century, but they would recover before too long.

The clock was ticking and Langley urgently needed to find out more about Gussage St Vincent's DIABOLICAL PLAN, so he lifted his left leg to complete the complicated but highly effective HUSH-HUSH-LUSH-GUSH Pose and continued his observations.

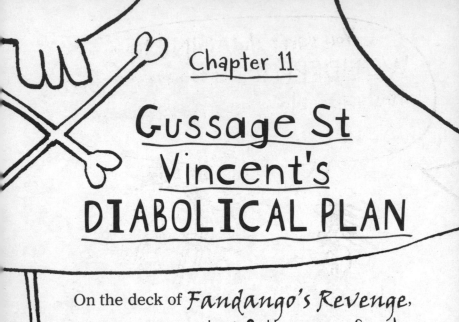

Chapter 11

Gussage St Vincent's DIABOLICAL PLAN

On the deck of *Fandango's Revenge*, Gussage strode gleefully over to Scawby Briggs, who was leaning over the railings at the side of the ship.

"At last," he said, giving his GREAT, great, great, *great*, great, great, GREAT, great, great, great, great, great, GREAT, great, great, great, great, GREAT, great, great, GREAT, great, *great*, great, GREAT, great, GREAT, <u>GREAT</u> <u>GRANDSON</u> a great big SLAP on the back.

"A MINOR DETAIL," yelled Gussage as he pranced around the deck until he reached the **W.A.T.CH.** power unit. Smoke was pouring out of it…and the usually black **W.A.T.CH.** was now so red that it looked as though it was about to EXPLODE at any minute.

"It's probably something to do with this temporary power unit we installed. **W.A.T.CH.**es weren't designed to transport whole ships through TIME you know!"

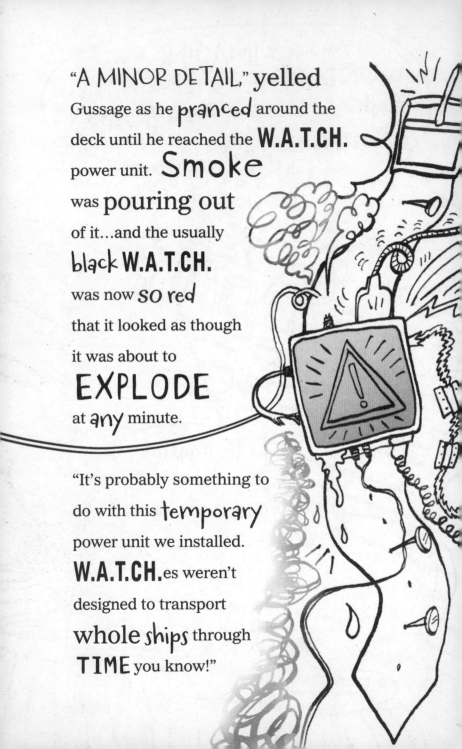

Despite the horrendous whiff coming from the

MUCKSLOWE MURPHY'S
Caskets o' Fun

Langley adopted the **BOLIVIAN NOSE-HOLDING Pose** and looked on from the safety of the shadows.

Gussage held his hand up to his eyes and peered at the sun.

"Hmmmm," he said. "It seems as long as the ship is powered by a **W.A.T.CH.**, we'll only get about fifteen minutes of **TIME TRAVEL** in any one journey."

"Aye, Master," said Jinxy LaBabbage again.

"And by the look of that there **W.A.T.CH.**, we'll need to do a spot of repair work before we set sail again," Jinxy went on.

"Maybe these will help – I spotted them just lying around as we left the prison," smiled Gussage as he pulled a couple of **W.A.T.CH.**es out of his pocket. "They looked so sad and alone that I thought I'd bring them back and put them to good use."

Gussage tossed one of the **W.A.T.CH.**es to Jinxy LaBabbage.

Don't worry, I've turned off the **FPU** tracking device that ALL **W.A.T.CH.**es have. They WON'T have a clue WHERE we are.

BRILLIANT, Master, I'll get Nigel and Two-planks to replace the old **W.A.T.CH.** If anyone can get it done quick sharp, it's those two.

"EXCELLENT," said Gussage. "And while they're doing that I shall run over my plans with you again. This time, NOTHING will go wrong."

Feeling a bit better, Jinxy LaBabbage smiled and moved closer to Gussage.

"Aye aye, Master," he said. "So what's next?"

Once again, Gussage reached into his pocket and this time pulled out a small, blinking InfoStor device.*

"Whilst, I confess, it is simply SUPER to have Scawby on board with me, getting him out was a teeny bit of a diversion. You see, I needed to access the FPU database and I knew that the best place to do that would be from a computer inside the prison. All the guards would be busy trying to stop you from freeing Scawby and so I could work uninterrupted.

* The InfoStor is an INFOrmation STORage device that works a bit like a twenty-first century memory stick.

My plan worked PERFECTLY and I found exactly what I needed."

Watching from the shadows, Langley had NEVER heard such a DASTARDLY plan. In fact, what he was hearing was SO alarming that he had unknowingly assumed the **STREATHAM SHOCKER pose**.

"You see," continued Gussage. "I knew the **FPU** would have analysed Compton Valance's TIME MACHINE SANDWICH to try and work out its chemical make-up, so ALL the information I need is RIGHT HERE. I don't need the sandwich itself to create my EXTRAORDINARY TIME-TRAVELLING PIRATE GALLEON. I just need to TRAVEL THROUGH TIME to, er, pilfer a few items that will recreate the sandwich's chemical recipe."

Jinxy LaBabbage's eyes ⚡LIT UP⚡ when he heard the word "pilfer". If there was one thing he loved doing more than anything else in the world it was a LOVELY SPOT OF PILFERING.

So, where are we goin' first? he asked.

Well, the sandwich is flavoured with cheese and pickled egg, and according to the FPU's chemical breakdown, the pickled egg bit can be recreated by using particles found in a now EXTINCT variety of Asian chilli pepper. So WHEN the power supply is functioning again we shall set sail to sixteenth-century India to find some.

Gussage strode back to Scawby, who was **still** bent over the railings by the side of the main deck.

"Aye aye, Master," said Jinxy LaBabbage.

"And while we go there, young Scawby here will

TRAVEL BACK to the FUTURE,"

said Gussage, smiling a horrid smile. "I have another little job for him."

And with that Gussage laughed a hearty and OUTRAGEOUSLY EVIL laugh as he thrust the other **W.A.T.CH.** and a hooded cloak into Scawby's arms.

"Mwhah hah ha ha haa!!"

Jinxy LaBabbage joined in and laughed along with his master.

"Ha-ha ha-ha! Ha ha!!"

And as Gussage and Jinxy LaBabbage
laughed their EVIL laughs,

Mwhah hah ha ha!!
Mwhah hah ha ha haaa!!!

Ha-ha,
haaa!

Scawby was *sick* over the side of the ship, *again*.

Ha Ha hah...
Huh, huh...
Ha ha ha
HAAA!!

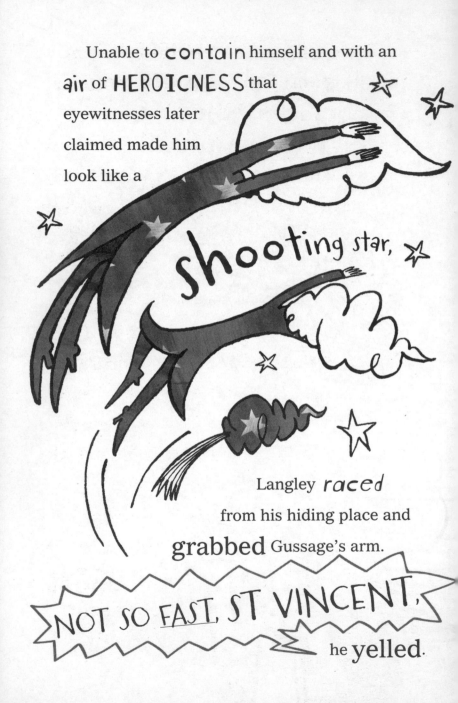

Unable to **contain** himself and with an **air** of **HEROICNESS** that eyewitnesses later claimed made him look like a **shooting** star, Langley *raced* from his hiding place and **grabbed** Gussage's arm.

NOT SO FAST, ST VINCENT, he **yelled**.

"You're **not** going ANYWHERE. I hereby **arrest** you in the name of the **FPU**. **You**, *sir*, are going back to PRISON." Langley pushed a button on his **W.A.T.CH.** and waited for the air to crackle and f1zz. Unfortunately though, the air on *Fandango's Revenge* *didn't* crackle or f1zz. He looked at his **W.A.T.CH.** and saw that it had a big crack down the middle of it. It had been damaged during all the tossing and spinning they'd done when they'd travelled back from the twenty-seventh century.

Gussage stroked his COLOSSAL moustache with delight.

Future Perfect Unit

File (088763)

CHEMICAL BREAKDOWN OF THE
COMPTON VALANCE TIME MACHINE SANDWICH

▶ **PRELIMINARY NOTES** ◀

THIS CHEMICAL ANALYSIS OF THE TIME MACHINE
SANDWICH WAS PERFORMED BY DR OXYGEN, PROFESSOR
GLYN CAIROG AND THE COMPUTERIZED ROBOT, MARK.

Composition of sandwich:

> It is noted that the "sandwich" is comprised
of four main areas of interest:

1. Bread

2. Egg (pickled)

3. Cheese
(Sleeton Bassett's
Extra Extra Extra
Strong Cheddar)

4. Outer Crust
(this thick
fungal layer
has built up
over time
and was NOT
part of the
original
design of
the sandwich)

1. The bread:

> During the course of its life, the "sandwich" has sustained massive discolouration of the bread. In fact, the bread now seems to change colour on a fairly regular basis.

> During the analysis period the sandwich changed from brown to weird brown, to really weird brown to green to yellow to blue to a sort of rainbow colour, to purple and back to brown.

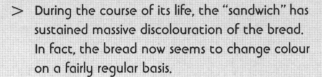

> The usual traces of flour, yeast, water and sugar were found in addition to very high quantities of particles found in a now extinct variety of chilli pepper, most often associated with cooking in the Maharashtra region of India in the mid-sixteenth century.

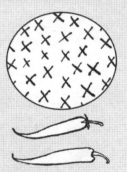

2. The egg (pickled):

> Usual amounts of water, proteins and fats detected.

> However, over time (possibly due to the presence of strong pickling vinegar), some of the egg particles had changed and mutated genetically.

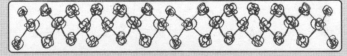

> The ones found by
  Dr Oxygen and MARK
  resembled particles found
  in a rare variety of apple
  that has then been bruised
  by a bewigged head.

3. The cheese:

> It is the chemical make-up of the cheese that has
  changed most dramatically.

> The core temperature of the cheese in the middle
  of the sandwich was nearly 300°C (although this
  may have been due to Professor Cairog
  putting it in the oven
  when she accidentally
  mistook it for
  her lunch).

> The chemistry of the cheese
  now more closely resembles
  the two-thousand-year-old
  skin and sweat cells of a
  human male who has
  recently performed a HUGE
  amount of exercise in close
  proximity to horses and a
  massive crowd of people.

4. The outer crust (OC)

> This has been the most difficult element of the sandwich to analyse.

> The number of times it has been used to travel through time has severely compromised the original integrity of the sandwich's crust.

> Upon analysis it was found that the OC contains several batches of human DNA. These have been identified as DNA from the people who have bitten into the sandwich, namely:

Compton Valance,

Bryan Nylon

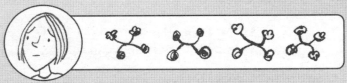

and Bravo Valance.

Chapter 12

A Hair-raising Experience

The air in The Commissioner's super-secret office crackled and fizzed again and Langley Von Tinklehorn

APPEARED,

immediately assuming the **RETURNING HERO** Pose.

"How did you get here?" said Compton who, only five minutes earlier, had seen Langley DISAPPEAR on a spinning, flying, PIRATE-SHIP TIME MACHINE and who, only thirty seconds before, had seen The Commissioner open a letter that Langley had sent because he was trapped in the eighteenth century.

Langley Von Tinklehorn placed his clenched **fist** under his **stubbly chin**, completing the **THOUGHTFUL HERO 2.0 Pose**.

It's a l o n g story, he said.

But basically I travelled back to the year 1732, where I tried to ARREST Gussage St Vincent but couldn't as my **W.A.T.CH.** had been damaged. He then CAPTURED me, TIED me to the mast of *Fandango's Revenge* while we sailed to a deserted island. I was then UNTIED, MARCHED onto the island and LEFT for DEAD.

Thankfully, a few hours later a trading ship just HAPPENED to be passing the deserted island and I was able to get their attention by JUMPING up and down and SHOUTING a lot. After I was PICKED UP it took just over three months to get back to England, where I IMMEDIATELY wrote a letter to The Commissioner, with very SPECIFIC instructions for it to be delivered TODAY.

That's right, said The Commissioner.

As soon as I got the letter I SENT a **Recovery Squad** back to the eighteenth century to PICK HIM UP and GIVE him a new **W.A.T.CH.**

"Wow," said Bryan. "That's pretty cool."

"Yes it is!" said Langley Von Tinklehorn, jumping up **suddenly** into the **HEROIC ACTION Pose #19.**

But what is more AMAZING is that I KNOW WHAT Gussage's plan is.

Almost without realizing it, Compton and Bryan adopted the **HEROIC ACTION Pose #19** too.

"What is his plan?" said The Commissioner.

He has TAKEN a file from the FPU database that lists the chemical make-up of Compton and Bryan's TIME MACHINE SANDWICH,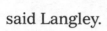

said Langley.

He has rigged up a W.A.T.CH. to POWER Fandango's Revenge and is using it to TRAVEL THROUGH TIME to collect the things that he needs. The W.A.T.CH. ONLY gives him a small window of TIME-TRAVEL TIME though. That's WHY the ship was so out of control when we saw it.

"So he *doesn't* have a fully functioning **TIME MACHINE**?" said Bryan.

"Not **yet**," said Langley.

"Well," said The Commissioner. "That gives us a chance to stop him before he does."

"The last I heard, he was about to go to India, some time in the sixteenth century," said Langley.

The Commissioner searched for the file on her *InfoTab*.

It says he needs an EXTINCT variety of chilli pepper,

she said.

But there's NO way we could be sure EXACTLY what moment of what day in a WHOLE century he'll be going back to.

"So **what** do we do *now*?" said Compton.

The Commissioner walked over to her **HUGE** window and looked down on **New New London** seventy-two floors below.

"I'll give this information to the **FPU Agents** in the **HUSH-HUSH TOP SECRET OPERATIONS ROOM** and they will let us know if they discover anything in any of the **TIMELINES**."

Everyone nodded in agreement.

"But it's **unbelievably IMPORTANT** that **no one** outside this room discovers what's really going on," she said. "People would panic if they knew that Gussage St Vincent was **still alive** and trying to become the

MASTER OF TIME AND OVERLORD OF THE UNIVERSE."

The Commissioner ran her fingers through her long, wavy hair.

Compton and Bryan, I want YOU to go back to the F. A. R. T. Academy. Your PHASE TWO TRAINING begins tomorrow morning and it is VITAL that you start it as normal. You two are so FAMOUS that if you DIDN'T turn up, people would ask questions. We don't want people thinking that ANYTHING is wrong.

Compton and Bryan nodded.

But while you are in the F. A. R. T. Academy I want YOU to be MY eyes and ears,

continued The Commissioner.

If Gussage makes **ANY** changes to HISTORY, no matter **HOW** tiny, these changes will have an effect on the **PRESENT**. If he takes something from – or does something in – the **PAST**, that will create a slightly different **TIMELINE** to the one that would have existed. *Understand?*

Compton and Bryan nodded.

Coming, as **YOU** do, from our **PAST**, you'll be able to notice these changes **BETTER** than anyone. If **YOU** spot anything **STRANGE**, just call me on your **HandPhone**.

We **HAVEN'T** got **HandPhone**s,

said Compton.

"Oh, **sorry**, I should have **explained**," said The Commissioner. "We have a **special Wi-Fi** at the **FPU** that automatically turns your hands into **HandPhones**."

Compton and Bryan stared at the palms of their hands.

"If you **need** to get hold of me, push **twice** just below your little **finger**."

Compton looked at Bryan and then pushed just below his little **finger**. The Commissioner's **HandPhone** started to **ring**.

Hello?

she said, answering the call.

Compton s l o w l y put his **thumb** up to his **ear** and spoke into his little **finger**.

Er, hello?

he said.

"You see," said The Commissioner, still talking into her little finger. "It's that simple. Just hang up by pushing hard right in the middle of your palm."

"COOL!" said Compton. "How do we order pizza?"

The Commissioner decided to ignore this comment. "Now REMEMBER, you must act completely naturally and tell absolutely NO ONE what you are up to, but let us know the second you notice any change, however tiny. We are relying on you both. THE FUTURE OF THE HUMAN RACE MAY DEPEND UPON IT."

As The Commissioner spoke, the air in her office crackled and fizzed for the shortest fraction of a second...

Compton and Bryan looked at each other
and then back at The Commissioner.

"Er, we **think** we *might*
have spotted the first
change," said Compton.

"What?" said The
Commissioner.

"Er, you and Langley
seem to have swapped
hairdos."

The Commissioner
touched her hair and
sure enough, she had a
stacked, white
ice-cream-whip
hairstyle.

Chapter 13

The Fearless Bandit Strikes AGAIN!

Compton and Bryan sat at the saloon table. Ol' Doc Charro sat opposite, chewing the end of a toothpick. He narrowed his eyes and placed the three of diamonds onto the pack at the centre of the table. Quick as a flash Compton smacked his hand down hard on top of the cards.

DOGDARN!

yelled Ol' Doc, smiling.

Ya plumb licked me, ya young caboose.

Compton smiled back, picked up the cards from the table and placed them on the bottom of his stack. The saloon **erupted** in a **GREAT CHEER** and Ruby Montana came over and gave Compton a **HUGE hug** and a **kiss** on the cheek. The piano player in the corner of the room began another **loud** and **rousing** rendition of

YIPPEE YIPPEE YO (Got ME A NEW Spittoon).

As the **celebrations** continued, the doors
SMASHED OPEN
and there stood
The Fearless Bandit.

The piano playing **stopped**
and a **frightened** **hush**
fell over the **whole** saloon.

The Fearless Bandit peered from behind his black eye-mask and slowly walked inside. In his hand he held a custard pie.

The spurs on his heels made a slow clink clink clink clink as he stalked across the wooden floor and over to the bar. When he reached the long shiny counter, he turned to face the room.

ALL OF YOU CAN GIT,

he said, stroking his ENORMOUS moustache.

I'M ONLY HERE FOR VALANCE!

No one waited for a second invitation and the saloon EXPLODED with a

HUGE COMMOTION

as the rest of the customers ran for the door. Compton could see that The Fearless Bandit now had the custard pie in his throwing arm, ready for ACTION.

YOU GOT THREE SECONDS BEFORE I START A THROWIN',

he grinned, showing off his silver teeth. A loud rumbling noise cut through the tense quiet. Compton turned and saw that Bryan was fast asleep at the table and snoring loudly.

ZZZZZ...
ZZZ...

"Wake up, Bry!" he said, taking his eye **off** the Fearless Bandit and **shaking** the arm of his friend. Bryan didn't move.

BRYAN! he **yelled**.

WAKE UP!

Bryan didn't stir.

WAKE UP! WAKE UP! WAKE UP!

he **screamed**.

It was **too late**. The **full FORCE** of The Fearless Bandit's **custard pie** caught him in the face, **throwing** him backwards and out of the chair. Through mouthfuls of **custard** Compton kept **yelling**.

WAKE UP! WAKE UP!

Compton awoke with a start to find himself in his bedroom in the **F. A. R. T. Academy** with **IAN** yelling at him.*

* IAN stands for Information And News and is a twenty-seventh century HOLOGRAPHIC communications device that acts a bit like a TV, the internet and an organizer all in one. Oh, and a very, _very_ LOUD alarm clock!

Compton held up his hands.

"I'm awake, **IAN**, I'm awake," he said and stumbled out of bed. Compton was feeling very, *very* tired. He and Bryan had spent most of the night in The Commissioner's office looking at the file that Gussage had stolen.

They had gone over it then THAT way, THIS way, then the OTHER way, then a thousand DIFFERENT ways,

all the time searching for a clue about where and when Gussage would strike next.

The Commissioner had *even* put the file onto Compton and Bryan's InfoTabs. 179

But despite **all** their hard work, as Compton **wiped** the sleep out of his eyes, he felt **no** closer to knowing **anything new** about Gussage St Vincent.

Good morning – *buzz* – Compton Valance,

said **IAN**, flickering a little.

Today is the first day of PHASE TWO TRAINING. You **must** make your way to the Eating Zone for a welcome talk from Mr Susan Glanville – *buzz*.

Okay, **IAN**, okay,

said Compton as he slowly got used to being awake.

Wardrobe.

Compton's **wardrobe** *slid* out from
the wall and the doors opened to reveal
one **bright-red**, tight **F. A. R. T.
Academy** uniform, one
gold uniform and
his **backpack.** *

Five minutes
later he was
dressed and
ready and on
his way to the
Eating Zone.

* In the twenty-seventh century all rooms are FULLY automated. As soon as you say the name of the thing you want, it APPEARS.

181

He quickly found Bryan and they grabbed a table with Hector and Lola, their best friends from **PHASE ONE TRAINING**. It had only been a few months since Compton and Bryan had last been in the F. A. R. T. Academy but it seemed like they'd been away for much, *much* longer.

"It's great to see you two again," said Hector. "How was your summer?"

Compton kicked Bryan under the table and gave him an EVIL look. Unfortunately he tried to smile innocently at Hector and Lola at the same time, which just made him look like he had sat on a javelin.

"We're *supposed* to be acting like NOTHING is wrong," he whispered to Bryan.

Lola and Hector were just about to ask WHAT on earth was going on but before they could, Mr Susan Glanville, the head of the F. A. R. T. Academy,

crackled and fizzed onto a floating red disc that hovered in the middle of the room.

"WELCOME!" he boomed. "It's wonderful to see so many familiar faces as well as a few new ones."

For the next few minutes Compton didn't pay any attention to what Mr Susan Glanville was saying. He could have been talking in French about how to blow up a balloon using your knees for all Compton heard. *

No, Compton was too busy scanning the Eating Zone, looking for any changes that might have taken place because of Gussage St Vincent's meddlings with THE PAST. Out of the corner of his eye,

* He wasn't. He was simply running through a few things about the F.A.R.T. ACADEMY for the benefit of the new students.

184

Compton spotted Lola staring at him.

He smiled at her and quickly turned back to

Mr Susan Glanville as he delivered the final

part of his welcome speech.

And SO to your lessons, he said.

You will EACH find a copy of your timetable on your InfoTab. PHASE THREE students, you will see that you will begin your studies with Mr Bobson, who will take you to the **Time Museum** for a special lecture on the HISTORY OF THE **W.A.T.CH.** PHASE ONE students, you have a lesson on TIME PORTALS with the ROBOT Mr Milton Abbas. PHASE TWO students, you will begin your studies with Dr Bongo. You've got a WONDERFUL first day to look forward to with your first TIME-TRAVEL field trip.

Compton looked over at Bryan to see him using his *hands* like

to look around the room. Hector was staring at him.

"What is up with you two?" Hector said, before grabbing his backpack and getting up to go.

It was OBVIOUS that Compton and Bryan would have to put a *bit* more work into their "acting naturally" skills.

Chapter 14

The Greatest Lesson in the HISTORY of EVER

Dr Bongo had been leading TIME-TRAVEL field trips at the F. A. R. T. Academy for the last fifteen years. It was widely thought that he loved his lessons as much, if not more, than his students.

"TIME-TRAVEL field trips are a WONDERFUL way for Academy Agents to get used to TRAVELLING THROUGH TIME and encountering a range of different historic environments," he said, addressing the new PHASE TWO class. "Over the next twelve weeks we will witness some of the most fabulous and extraordinary events that have EVER happened and you will get to experience HISTORY first-hand."

Compton and Bryan sat at the back of the class in a state of EXTREME ALERTNESS, observing as much as possible. Compton couldn't help but think Dr Bongo's lessons were much more interesting than Strictly Strickland's.

"He's a bit odd-looking, isn't he?" said Bryan.

Compton nodded at Bryan's mastery of the understatement. The words "a bit odd-looking" did not even begin to fully convey Dr Bongo's ASTONISHING clothing choices.

"Apparently he brings a bit of clothing back with him whenever he time travels," he said.

Today their teacher was wearing an ENORMOUS sugarloaf hat that he had taken a shine to when he had visited the court of Queen Elizabeth in the year 1592, a T-shirt from 1984 that said "RELAX" and a pair of traditional golden, deep-fried trousers that he'd picked up in Glasgow in 2412.

So, WHO wants to know about your very first TIME-TRAVEL field trip?

said Dr Bongo, smiling.

A ripple of excitement fluttered around the classroom. Dr Bongo's TIME-TRAVEL field trips were the stuff of ABSOLUTE legend. Compton had heard that he'd once taken a class back to 1838 to watch Queen Victoria's coronation. Another time, he'd taken his **Academy Agents** back in time 104 million years to see a baby T. rex hatch. Last year, he'd even arranged a field trip back to 2094 to witness the first marriage between a human and a photocopier. *

* The marriage between Penelope Battelle and an Astoria 10-22-38 lasted for a very happy thirty-six years, until Penelope lost the manual for her husband and couldn't unblock a paper jam in tray four.

Dr Bongo pushed a button on his desk and a HOLOGRAM APPEARED in front of him, showing an ENORMOUS oval stadium, with seven horse-drawn chariots racing around the track. As Compton watched the hologram, a memory stirred right at the back of his brain.

This afternoon, we will be TRAVELLING BACK to AD 146 and visiting the ancient Roman stadium called CIRCUS MAXIMUS!

RELAX

A **HUGE** cry of **YES!** erupted in the classroom. Dr Bongo proceeded to tell the class all about ancient Rome to make sure they would be able to blend in.

Compton, Bryan and the rest of the **PHASE TWO** students discovered that ancient Romans washed their clothes in wee, that some Roman women wore the sweat of gladiators instead of perfume, and that, if they needed the toilets in the **CIRCUS MAXIMUS**, they would be expected to wipe their bottoms with a communal

SPONGE on a stick.*

* Use of the **communal bottom sponge** is a practice that found favour nearly **two thousand** years later in Bedfordshire. In fact, between the years 2021 and 2039, a sign that you passed on entering the county read: "WELCOME TO BEDFORDSHIRE, THE BUM-SPONGE COUNTY".

"But the most EXCITING part about this afternoon's TIME-TRAVEL trip I've saved until last," said Dr Bongo, with a smile.

He pushed the button on his desk again and a HOLOGRAM APPEARED of a man wearing a helmet and dressed in a white toga.

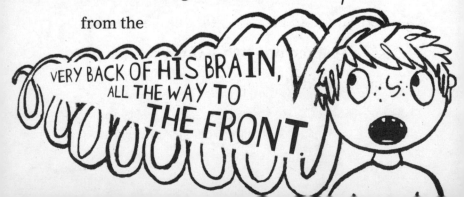

"This is Gaius Appuleius Diocles," said Dr Bongo, pointing towards the hologram. "The most successful charioteer of ALL TIME! This afternoon, for your first TIME-TRAVEL field trip, we are going to go and watch his FINAL race."

A great CHEER rang around the classroom and as it did, Compton's recently stirred memory started moving at tremendous speed from the

VERY BACK OF HIS BRAIN, ALL THE WAY TO THE FRONT.

"Now then," said Dr Bongo. "We need to go and get everyone a set of authentic Roman clothes so that we can properly blend in with the locals. Everyone follow me to the

Theodore Logan Memorial Hall and Reception Zone;

we have one more stop to make before we leave for Rome."

As they stood up to follow Dr Bongo and the rest of the **PHASE TWO** students out of the classroom, a thought flashed through Compton's brain.

"I think I know where Gussage will STRIKE next," he said, giving Bryan a sharp nudge in his ribs. "Remember the file he stole about our sandwich?"

Bryan nodded.

"It said that the cheese molecules from the sandwich resembled the two-thousand-year-old skin and sweat cells of a man who had been exercising heavily near horses and a large crowd."*

Bryan looked at Compton blankly.

"Don't you get it?" said Compton, pointing at the hologram of Gaius Appuleius Diocles.

Gussage St Vincent is the BIGGEST SHOW-OFF EVER. I think there's a VERY good chance that he'll want the skin and sweat cells of the MOST FAMOUS CHARIOTEER in HISTORY.

* It's true. You can go back and see for yourselves on page 157.

Chapter 15

Mr Beadle, Mr Beadle and Mr Beadle (Senior)

After reaching the

Theodore Logan Memorial Hall and Reception Zone,

Dr Bongo pushed a button on his **W.A.T.CH.** and a door

☆ materialized ☆

in front of the **PHASE**

TWO students.

"Where's Compton Valance?" he asked as he did a quick headcount of his excited students.

"I'm here," said Compton, catching up with the rest of the group.

"Please don't wander off," said Dr Bongo. "It's very IMPORTANT that we all stick together unless I instruct otherwise."

Compton had actually gone to make a call to The Commissioner on his HandPhone. He wanted to let her know as soon as possible where he thought Gussage would be.

"The Commissioner is going to send Langley and some FPU Agents along to capture Gussage at CIRCUS MAXIMUS," Compton whispered to Bryan. "She says that they'll be completely disguised and we probably won't even realize there's anyone there."

"**PHASE TWO** students," said Dr Bongo

GRANDLY, "before every trip **BACK IN TIME, F. A. R. T. Academy** students come here."

Dr Bongo gestured to the sign on the door. It said:

FPU C.A.M.O.*
DIVISION
DIRECTORS:
BEADLE, BEADLE
& BEADLE (SENIOR)

RELAX

* Concealment And Masking Outfitters

"Through this door," he continued, "are PERFECT replicas of EVERY kind of clothing worn at EVERY TIME in the HISTORY OF THE WORLD. In here, FPU agents can disguise themselves to blend in to any environment imaginable."

"*Every* kind of clothing?" said Suzanne Davois. "How can they do that?"

"Come with me and find out," smiled Dr Bongo and he walked through the door.

Compton, Bryan and the rest of the PHASE TWO students followed, and found themselves in a cavernous but completely

EMPTY

white room.

So where are all the clothes? said Compton, looking around. I can't see any.

A tiny, frail, unbelievably OLD man, with ear hair that was so long he was able to fashion it into a lovely warm scarf, mysteriously APPEARED.

Have you ANY idea HOW MUCH room it would take up to have EVERY single possible item of clothing from EVERY single possible time period in EVERY single possible size? We'd have NO room for ANYTHING else!

he snapped.

He's NOT Mr Beadle (Senior), young man,

said a feeble voice from above them. The PHASE TWO students looked up and, just above their heads, saw a man sitting in a hover chair who looked even OLDER than the first RIDICULOUSLY OLD man.

"Oh, er-er, I'm sorry, Mr Beadle (Senior)," said Compton, getting a bit flustered.

The hover chair s l o w l y descended and as it did the class was able to take in the full, shrivelled scale of the old man's face.

It was more PUCKERED than a dog's bottom and more wrinkly than a ten-thousand-year-old walnut that had *really* let itself go.

Oh, I'm NOT Mr Beadle (Senior) either,

he said, bashing as many shins as he could while manoeuvring his hover chair to get a really CLOSE look at Compton.

Mr Beadle (Senior) is over there.

He raised one of his matchstick thin arms and pointed to the other side of the room. As he did this, a circular trapdoor whooshed open and a GIGANTIC BLUE ROBOT started to rise out of the floor.

However, this was no *ordinary* GIGANTIC BLUE ROBOT. No, *this* GIGANTIC BLUE ROBOT had a HUGE glass jar where its head should have been. And inside that HUGE glass jar, swimming in some sort of bubbling liquid, was the head of an old, old, <u>old</u>, old, <u>OLD</u>, OLD man.

I'M Mr Beadle (Senior),

said the head in the jar.

And I'm DELIGHTED to welcome you to the FPU C.A.M.O. Division.

With that, Mr Beadle (Senior) CLANGED across the floor in his **powerful ROBOTIC LEGS**, towards the **PHASE TWO** students.

"Wonderful to see you again, Dr Bongo," he said, shaking his hand vigorously.

"And **when** will you be travelling to?"

"Ancient Rome, AD146," said Dr Bongo. "Is the DIZZY GENNY ready?"

Mr Beadle (Senior) smiled, or at least that's what it *looked* like he was doing – inside the liquid-filled glass jar it was quite difficult to tell.

"Oh, DIZZY is always ready for you," he said. "Would EVERYONE like to come with me?"

As the students followed the Mr Beadles and Dr Bongo across the floor and through a door marked

NOBODY noticed the door to the FPU C.A.M.O. DIVISION open...

...and a strange hooded figure skulk inside.

Chapter 16

The DIZZY GENNY

The **PHASE TWO** students found themselves standing on a SQUARE, SHINY white floor alongside a big, golden curtain. Compton looked at the curtain and wondered what could be behind it.

As he spoke, Mr Beadle (Senior) grabbed a **thick**, golden cord that hung at the side of the golden curtain.

"And ALL this is possible thanks to the MARK 4 DISGUISE GENERATOR, otherwise known as DIZZY GENNY."

Using one of his COLOSSAL ROBOTIC HAND PINCERS, Mr Beadle (Senior) yanked hard on the cord and the curtains SWWOOOSShhed to one side.

The PHASE TWO students gasped as they found themselves in front of a beautiful, SHINY, silver MACHINE that was as tall as a house. Mr Beadle (Senior) gently patted the side of DIZZY GENNY.

A hum of excitement babbled through the PHASE TWO students. Lola and Hector high-fived each other. Suzanne Davois and Phil Kokinos did a little happy dance. Bryan wondered if there'd be time to go for a wee before they left. *

"DIZZY GENNY works by using a HUGE database of clothing from history," said Mr Beadle (Senior), using his PINCER to push some of the lights on the front of the machine. As he did this, a screen flickered to life. "Here I simply select the TIME PERIOD and the kind of outfit we require. So let's set it to AD 146, Rome."

* If Bryan had one OVERALL complaint about TIME-TRAVELLING it was how easy it was to forget to go to the loo.

Mr Beadle (Senior) looked at Compton.

"Just **stand** on that **green circle** for me would you?"

Compton moved over and **stood** a bit **nervously** on the circle.

Er, does the DIZZY GENNY EVER get it wrong?

he asked.

Mr Beadle (Senior) kept pressing buttons.

"Oh, occasionally, *occasionally*," he said.

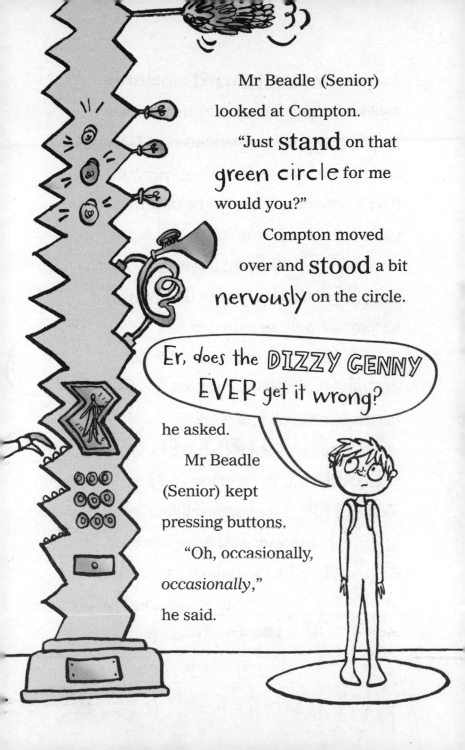

"Even the most POWERFUL computers make small mistakes from time to time. Nothing to worry about, nothing to worry about at all."

Compton was just about to raise the matter of WHY Samuel Nathaniel Daniels's attempts at disguises were so terrible, when a small drawer next to him on the DIZZY GENNY whirred open.

"Now then," said Mr Beadle (Senior). "DIZZY GENNY is linked to the FPU computer database that holds ALL the snot samples for BOGEY RECOGNITION TECHNOLOGY. We need a bogey from you so DIZZY can access all your measurements and your DNA sequence for a quick and painless clothing transfer."

Compton plucked a succulent bogey from his nose and placed it in the drawer.

The drawer **whirred** shut and three green lights lit up on the side of the DIZZY GENNY.

The ENORMOUS machine began to hum loudly and the green circle that Compton was standing on started to pulse. The air around him crackled and fizzed and a moment later Compton's red F. A. R. T. Academy uniform had been replaced with a purple toga and a long brown cloak.

That is AMAZING,

said Lola.

You look GREAT, Compton.

Compton blushed a little and stepped off the green circle.

"Right then," said Mr Beadle (Senior). "Who wants to go next?"

EVERYONE immediately put their hands up and started jumping about excitedly. As the jostling and hand-waving got more and more FRANTIC, Tony Chang accidentally knocked Scafell Nevis...

who accidentally fell into Tina Bizzle...

who BASHED Foxy Guardin...

who fell backwards...

and SMASHED into the HULKING blue, ROBOTIC frame of Mr Beadle (Senior).

The room fell SILENT and everyone turned to watch as Mr Beadle (Senior) rocked back on his ROBOTIC FEET for a moment. The whole world seemed to run in slow motion as the HUGE glass jar that held Mr Beadle (Senior)'s head tipped backwards... and forwards... before it finally toppled from the safety of his broad ROBOTIC SHOULDERS and fell to the ground, SMASHING INTO TINY, TINY PIECES.

Mr Beadle (Senior)'s head rolled around on the floor through puddles of sticky gloop before finally coming to rest.

Don't worry, said the head of Mr Beadle (Senior) cheerfully.

THIS happens a lot more often than you'd think. NOW can someone pass me a dustpan and brush and we'll get YOU LOT kitted out and on your way before you can say Skribble-de-pappap-rappa-plop-a-ding-dong.*

* "Skribble-de-pappap-rappa-plop-a-ding-dong" just happened to be the 2655 New New London entry in the Eurovision Song Contest and was Mr Beadle (Senior)'s FAVOURITE song (even though it came last).

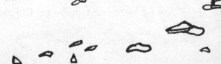

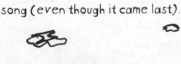

Chapter 17

CIRCUS MAXIMUS

Actually, due to a brief camouflage mishap with the DIZZY GENNY, it took everyone a little bit longer to get ready than it takes to say "Skribble-de-pappap-rappa-plop-a-ding-dong".*

However, less than twenty minutes after leaving the FPU C.A.M.O. DIVISION, the PHASE TWO students found themselves looking like real ancient Romans and standing round the back of one of the most FAMOUS BUILDINGS IN HISTORY.

* Mr Beadle (Senior) had accidentally knocked DIZZY GENNY with one of his powerful robotic pincers and changed the command "ancient Rome" to "ancient Gnome" resulting in Lotty Clare being camouflaged in dark green overalls with a LARGE red hat on her head and holding a fishing rod.

"This is the **CIRCUS MAXIMUS**," said Dr Bongo as he walked the **PHASE TWO** students round to the front of the **ENORMOUS** building. "The year is **AD 146** and this is a **stadium** where ordinary Roman citizens come to watch the **GREATEST** sporting spectacle of the age, chariot racing."

POOEEEEE! said Hector and Mo Lyon holding their noses. **WHAT is that STINK?**

Dr Bongo took a **deep** **sniff** of the ancient Roman air.

"Take your pick," he said, smiling and pointing at the Roman life all around them.

Ancient Romans WEREN'T as bothered about hygiene as you or I. LOOK, there's a BIG pile of sick over there by those steps.

Everyone looked at the big pile of sick.

URGH!

And it LOOKS very much to me as if a man is doing a POO right THERE in the street by his market stall.

Everyone looked at the man doing a POO by his market stall, then quickly looked away.

UUURRR-GGGHHH!!!

"Yuck," said Bryan. "Even I'm not allowed to do *that* in the street. Well, **not any more.**"

"Remember that as **TIME TRAVELLERS** it is **vital** that we blend in to our surroundings," said Dr Bongo. "You **must act** as though doing a poo in the street is **ENTIRELY normal.**"

A collective shudder went through the PHASE TWO students.

Compton nudged Bryan and pointed to a large, round man wearing a laurel wreath, on top of which sat a bowler hat that was three sizes too small. Passers-by were looking at him and laughing at his strange appearance.

Look! Compton whispered, trying to keep a straight face.

That MUST be one of the FPU agents who The Commissioner said we WOULDN'T notice.

The DIZZY GENNY MUST have been having a bit of an off day, sniggered Bryan.

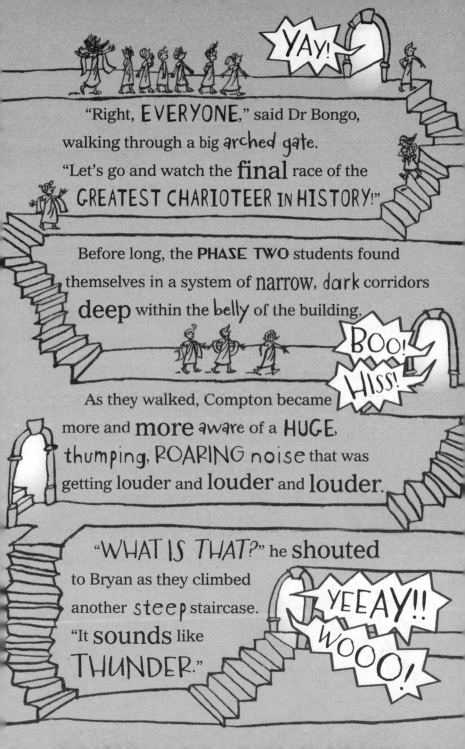

"Right, EVERYONE," said Dr Bongo, walking through a big arched gate. "Let's go and watch the final race of the GREATEST CHARIOTEER IN HISTORY!"

Before long, the PHASE TWO students found themselves in a system of narrow, dark corridors deep within the belly of the building.

As they walked, Compton became more and more aware of a HUGE, thumping, ROARING noise that was getting louder and louder and louder.

"WHAT IS THAT?" he shouted to Bryan as they climbed another steep staircase. "It sounds like THUNDER."

YAY!

BOO! HISS!

YEEAY!! WOOO!

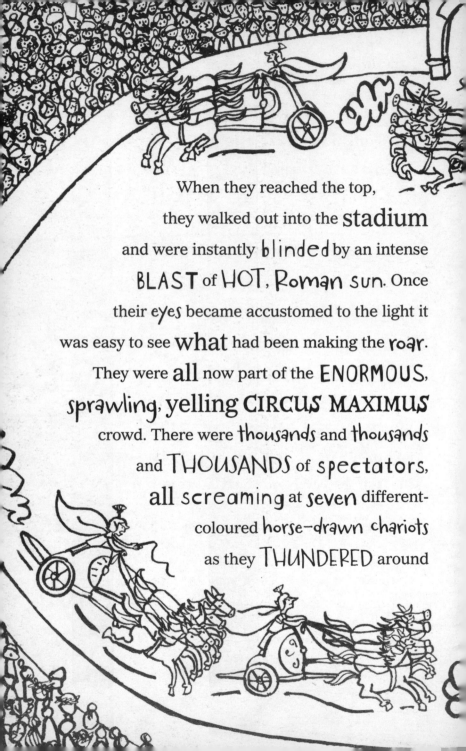

When they reached the top,
they walked out into the stadium
and were instantly blinded by an intense
BLAST of HOT, Roman sun. Once
their eyes became accustomed to the light it
was easy to see what had been making the roar.
They were all now part of the ENORMOUS,
sprawling, yelling CIRCUS MAXIMUS
crowd. There were thousands and thousands
and THOUSANDS of spectators,
all screaming at seven different-
coloured horse-drawn chariots
as they THUNDERED around

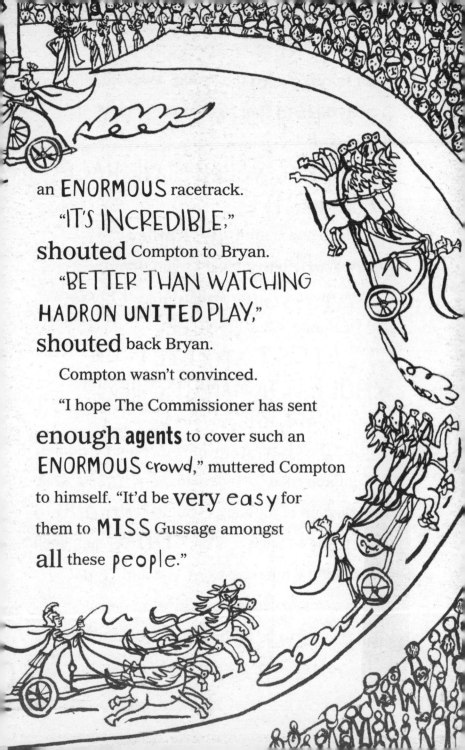

an ENORMOUS racetrack.
"IT'S INCREDIBLE,"
shouted Compton to Bryan.
"BETTER THAN WATCHING
HADRON UNITED PLAY,"
shouted back Bryan.

Compton wasn't convinced.

"I hope The Commissioner has sent
enough agents to cover such an
ENORMOUS crowd," muttered Compton
to himself. "It'd be very easy for
them to MISS Gussage amongst
all these people."

Dr Bongo guided the **PHASE TWO** students to an amazing spot right at the front of the crowd.

"LOOK," he yelled. "THE RACE HAS STARTED."

"Which one is the Guy Appley Diamondthingy bloke?" said Bryan.

"You mean Gaius Appuleius Diocles?" said Dr Bongo. "The SINGLE GREATEST ATHLETE IN THE WHOLE OF HUMAN HISTORY?"

"Er, yeah, him," said Bryan.

"He's the charioteer in red," said Dr Bongo.

Compton tried to understand exactly what was going on in the race but it was really difficult because EVERYTHING happened so fast. By the time the seventh and final lap was announced, a charioteer wearing blue seemed to be in the lead but behind him, a charioteer in red was gaining ground.

"Look," Compton said. "It's that Gaius bloke. He's *nearly* at the front."

The pair were neck and neck by the time they went into the final turn. As they entered the finishing straight Gaius Appuleius Diocles got his chariot as close as possible to the other chariot and PUSHED the blue charioteer to the ground.

One section of the crowd started booing and another erupted in cheers and applause.

"HE CHEATED!" yelled Bryan. "HE SHOULD BE SENT OFF! REF...? REF...?"

They watched as Gaius Appuleius Diocles crossed the finishing line and waved to the crowd in jubilation.

"The rules of chariot racing were a little, er, more rough than we're used to," smiled Dr Bongo.

"So he won his final race?" said Compton.

"He certainly did," said Dr Bongo. "Look at him now! Winning charioteers were treated like SUPERSTARS."

Gaius Appuleius Diocles got down from his chariot and bowed to the crowd. Compton and Bryan watched as hundreds of men and women swarmed around, hugging him and patting him on the back.

"Right then," said Dr Bongo. "I'm off to get a honeyed dormouse. Who wants one?"

As Dr Bongo took the rest of the PHASE TWO students off to see what other horrific snacks ancient Rome had to offer, Compton and Bryan decided to stay behind and inspect the presentation ceremony for any sign of Gussage St Vincent. Down on the track, a well-dressed, ENORMOUSLY fat man in a white cloak presented Gaius Appuleius Diocles with a HUGE bag of money. Compton scanned the crowd, trying to see if there were any FPU agents nearby. He couldn't see any but then he thought he spotted Langley Von Tinklehorn. It looked like someone near the toilets was performing the CLASSIC ACTION Pose #4.

"Where's Gussage?" whispered
Bryan. "He should be *here*."
Suddenly, a flashing
LIGHT caught Compton's eye
as the fierce afternoon sun
glinted off something metallic
in the crowd of people that had
surrounded the charioteer.

GOT HIM,

said Compton, shielding his eyes
from the glare. "He's down there."
Compton pointed towards the other side of
the stadium, about
a hundred
metres away.

Walking up to Gaius Appuleius Diocles was a man with a STUPENDOUS moustache and a mouth full of GLEAMING, silver teeth.

"Brilliant," said Bryan. "Now let's just sit back and watch the FPU agents GET him."

Compton and Bryan continued to watch Gussage St Vincent for a little longer. He began to chat to Gaius Appuleius Diocles and then walked with him over to the far side of the track.

"**Where** are the **agents**?" said Compton looking **frantically** around the **stadium** for signs of the **FPU**.

"He's going to **get away** if they don't **stop** him soon," said Bryan.

Compton **gritted** his **teeth**. They were **too close** now to let Gussage St Vincent **ESCAPE**. Without thinking, he grabbed Bryan and **pulled** him towards the track.

Come on,

he said, **leaping** over the barrier and into the **arena**.

We'll HAVE to catch him OURSELVES!

232

Chapter 18

A Few Minutes Earlier...

Gussage St Vincent was about as **happy** as a **hot monkey** stuck in a **barrel** of jam. His **unhappiness** could be broken down into **three** main areas.

1. His **beloved** *Fandango's Revenge* was still undergoing **repairs** after their trip back to **sixteenth-century India** and he had been **forced** to travel to **ancient Rome** using a **W.A.T.CH.** Even though he **knew** from past experience about the way changing **THE PAST** can affect **THE FUTURE,**

he'd been *really* looking forward to APPEARING out of nowhere, in a flying pirate ship in front of so many people.

2. The ancient Romans seemed to find his luxuriant moustache *exceptionally* funny.

He had already received several very strange looks from the locals.

3. He'd had to leave his MAGNIFICENT new pair of green and gold TRAVELLING trousers with ornamental stripes and HI-VIS safety flaps onboard ship because Jinxy LaBabbage had advised him they would attract too much attention.

So here he was, Gussage St Vincent, would-be MASTER OF TIME and three-time WINNER of MOUSTACHE OWNER OF THE YEAR, fizzing and

MOUSTACHE OWNER of the YEAR

crackling into the CIRCUS MAXIMUS wearing a stupid white toga and sandals.

"Right, Gussage, let's get the next item on the list and get out of this MASSIVE STENCH-HOLE," he said to himself as he looked down at the racetrack. He had arrived just in time to see Gaius Appuleius Diocles push his rival to the ground before crossing the finishing line and waving to the crowd.

Jolly, JOLLY GOOD,

said Gussage, applauding the SPECTACULAR display of bad behaviour. "I do SO LOVE a CHEAT."

He pulled out an ENORMOUS bag and gave it a shake. The gold coins inside gave a pleasing jangle. Gussage grinned and made his way down to the track. He was always pleasantly surprised at how little you needed to say when you were carrying a HUGE sack of cash.

He clapped his arm around Gaius Appuleius Diocles, showed him the BIG pouch of coins and ushered him over to a secluded corner of the track where he could conduct his business in private. Gussage switched on his W.A.T.CH.'s translation app.

I would like to BUY your UNDERGARMENTS,

he said loudly and s l o w l y into the W.A.T.CH.

Volo emere subligar tuum,

said the W.A.T.CH. and Gussage smiled encouragingly.

Luckily for Gussage this **wasn't** the first time that the charioteer had been asked this question after a **race** and so he gladly **removed** his **pants** and took the **cash**.

Insanis, said the charioteer, laughing and wandering off clutching the **money pouch**.

Subligaculum meum os asini obolet. HA HA HA HA.

You are **crazy**, repeated the **W.A.T.CH.**

My pants smell like the mouth of a donkey! HA HA HA HA.

Gussage smiled and held the charioteer's STINKY pants between his thumb and forefinger.

EXCELLENT, he murmured, keeping his face as far away from the pants as possible.

ANOTHER item ticked off the list.

He was just thinking how much they whiffed like a putrid slab of French brie, when he caught sight of Compton and Bryan rushing over to him from the other side of the track.

"What the...?" he said, stumbling back further into the shadows. "How on earth did they find me?"

As he watched he saw that Langley Von Tinklehorn had joined Compton and Bryan in

their *dash* across the **CIRCUS MAXIMUS**.
A *torrent* of fruity and colourful
words issued forth from Gussage's mouth.

I thought I'd got RID of that
jerrymumbling bog orange when
I left him on that DESERT ISLAND!

he said.

Blast ALL
of their
TOPLIGHTS!
I will NOT be
stopped by two
stupid ten year olds
and that gangling,
great SWIZZLETIFF.
NOT when I only need to get
one more item to turn *Fandango's
Revenge* into a PROPER
TIME-TRAVELLING
GALLEON.

As he grabbed his **W.A.T.CH.**, ready to transport himself back to his ship, a wicked idea began to swirl around his ENORMOUS brain.

"Although," he muttered to himself, "this might be a chance to take out a little insurance policy."

Compton, Bryan and Langley kept coming towards him at full tilt and were now so close that they were within earshot.

"Oh no," said Gussage very loudly as he retreated around a nearby corner. Compton, Bryan and Langley followed him with great speed, but when they turned the corner they stopped DEAD in their tracks. The air appeared to be crackling and fizzing a bit and Gussage St Vincent was nowhere to be seen.

"We've missed him!" said Langley breathing heavily, as he put his hands on his knees and assumed the **KNACKERED HERO** Pose.

"We were so close!" said Compton.

Just then, the air next to Compton crackled and fizzed and Gussage St Vincent APPEARED for a second. He grinned and grabbed Compton's arm.

Before Bryan or Langley could do anything about it, the air crackled and fizzed and Gussage and Compton DISAPPEARED.

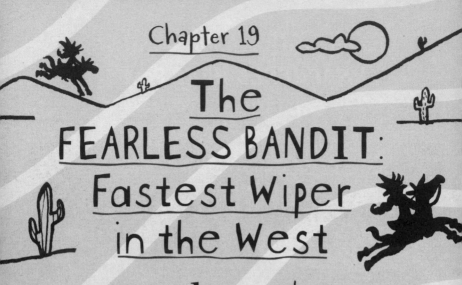

Chapter 19
The FEARLESS BANDIT: Fastest Wiper in the West

At the end of a **long** day in the saddle, Compton and Bryan sat around the campfire toasting marshmallows. The sun was low in the sky but there was just **enough LIGHT** for Compton to spot **someone** riding a horse in the distance.

"Who's *that?*" said Bryan, holding his hand up to his eyes to shield them from the sun.

Compton and Bryan looked
around for their horses but their
horses had VANISHED.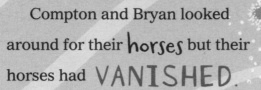
They were out in the open with
nowhere to hide. They watched as
The Fearless Bandit rode closer and
closer and closer. After a while he
reached Compton and Bryan's campsite and
jumped down from his horse.

I'VE GOT YOU NOW,

he roared and pulled a long
stick out from his jacket.
A stick with a sponge
attached to the end.

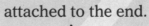

"What's *that?*" said Compton **nervously**.

The Fearless Bandit grinned so that Compton could see his **silver teeth**.

"Oh **you'll see**," he said and **shoved** the **sponge** bit of the **stick** down the back of his **trousers**.

> It's a COMMUNAL BOTTOM SPONGE!

said Compton, turning to Bryan.

Bryan **wasn't listening** though, he was **admiring** the lovely **toga** that he was wearing all of a sudden.

The Fearless Bandit pulled out the communal bottom sponge and held it up to Compton's face.

"NO!" yelled Compton who suddenly found himself POWERLESS to move.

The Fearless Bandit stepped towards him, communal bottom sponge outstretched, getting closer and closer.

NO! NO! NO!

yelled Compton as he felt the COLD, damp, clammy, STINKY communal bottom sponge

wafting under his nose.

 **URGH,** yelled Compton, as he **woke up** in a **daze**. He could see **someone** looming over him, holding a **damp rag.**

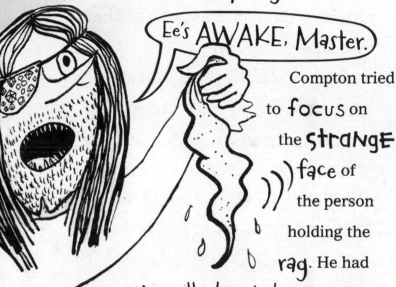 Ee's **AWAKE, Master.**

Compton tried to **focus** on the **strange** face of the person holding the **rag**. He had a jewelled **patch** over **one** eye and a **DISGUSTING** mouth crammed **full** of **nasty brown teeth.** "**EXCELLENT,**" said a **horribly familiar voice** from the back of the room. "Now **DO** help our **GUEST** up, Jinxy."

Compton felt his head and shoulders being lifted and then found himself sitting upright on a small bed in a gloomy, bare, wooden room. He could feel the bed roll gently and, outside, Compton heard the sound of seagulls.

"WHERE am I?" said Compton. "WHAT'S going on, St Vincent?"

"Welcome aboard Fandango's Revenge," said Gussage. "I thought you might like a look around. I'm afraid that you BUMPED your head when we landed and have been out like a LIGHT ever since."

WHAT are you going to DO with me?

said Compton, rubbing a bruise on the back of his head.

Chapter 20

The EXTRAORDINARY Wisdom of a Boy Named Bryan

Bryan, Langley Von Tinklehorn, Samuel Nathaniel Daniels and The Commissioner all stood in her secret office hidden behind a door in the FPU HQ marked

WOMEN'S TOILETS

OUT OF ORDER.

Well, Langley Von Tinklehorn, Samuel Nathaniel Daniels, The Commissioner and someone who looked a bit like Bryan stood in the office.

But instead of his usual mop of hair, this Bryan had a kind of slicked-back ponytail that sat proudly on top of his head. This Bryan was also wearing a silk dressing gown patterned with pictures of swirling dragons, and a pair of wooden sandals.*

* One of the results of Gussage St Vincent getting the sweat and skin cells of a Roman charioteer was that Bryan had CHANGED. He was now known as Bryan-san and was one of the GREATEST EXPERTS in the way of the ancient Japanese warrior class, the samurai. In fact, over three hundred million people had tuned in to see the first episode of his new TV show, 101 Ways To Smash Things With Your Head.

"We've got to **find Compton**," said Samuel Nathaniel Daniels, **pacing** the room and rubbing his **hands** together. Bryan sat **cross-legged** on The Commissioner's desk and **closed** his eyes.

By three methods we may learn WISDOM,

he said.

First, by REFLECTION, which is noblest. Second, by IMITATION, which is easiest. Third, by EXPERIENCE, which is bitterest. Reflection and experience will tell us WHERE Compton will be.

COMMISSIONER

After he had finished he bowed deeply to Samuel Nathaniel Daniels.

Bryan-san is RIGHT,

said The Commissioner.

Compton is going to be wherever Gussage is next. We KNOW he's got the extinct chilli pepper, the skin and sweat cells and he'll DEFINITELY have Compton's DNA by now. There's ONLY one thing left that he needs.

The rare variety of APPLE,

said Langley Von Tinklehorn.

"Do we have *any* ideas what *variety* it might **be**?" Bryan **breathed** deeply.

> Real KNOWLEDGE comes from knowing how little we KNOW. And yet the little we do KNOW might amount to EVERYTHING.

Langley Von Tinklehorn **clapped** his **hands** together. "Of COURSE," he said. "You're **completely right** *again*, Bryan-san. **What** do we **already KNOW** about the **variety** of **apple** that Gussage is going after?"

The Commissioner pulled up the **file** of the **chemical breakdown** of Compton and Bryan's **TIME MACHINE SANDWICH** on her *InfoTab*.

But being able to identify such an apple from the WHOLE of human history is IMPOSSIBLE,

said Samuel Nathaniel Daniels.

He's right,

said The Commissioner, her shoulders slumping at the thought of the task ahead of them.

Bryan opened his eyes and looked at The Commissioner, Samuel Nathaniel Daniels and Langley Von Tinklehorn in turn.

Those who conquer themselves are the MIGHTIEST warriors,

he said and shut his eyes again.

The previous actions of Gussage St Vincent will reveal his next move.

Of course,

said Langley.

Once again your WISDOM has shone a light, Bryan-san. Gussage takes the most FAMOUS item he can lay his hands on, doesn't he? Like in ancient Rome, an ORDINARY charioteer wasn't good enough, he HAD to have the sweat from the most SUCCESSFUL rider in HISTORY.

So he's going to get the most FAMOUS apple in HISTORY?

said Samuel Nathaniel Daniels.

But what's the most FAMOUS apple in HISTORY?

Silence is a true friend who NEVER betrays,

said Bryan in a whisper.

Search your mind, dear Samuel, the answer is deep within.

Sir Isaac Newton's apple!

said Samuel Nathaniel Daniels after a moment, as the penny dropped like, well, very much like an apple falling from a tree and onto a person's head due to the effect of GRAVITY.

Gussage will go after the apple that fell on Sir Isaac Newton's head.

Bryan uncrossed his legs and jumped down from the table. He grabbed a comb from his back pocket and ran it through his slicked-back hair. "Everyone ready?" he said. "Let's go get my best friend!"

The Commissioner pushed a button on her W.A.T.CH., the air in the room crackled and fizzed and EVERYONE DISAPPEARED.

Chapter 21

Tuesday 16th September 1666

The late summer sun bathed the gardens of Woolsthorpe Manor in a warm, golden light. Dressed in his casual mid-week afternoon outfit of shirt, cravat, waistcoat, trousers, jacket, highly-polished boots and a HUGE wig perched on top of his head, Sir Isaac Newton sat underneath a large Flower Of Kent apple tree, his back set against the stout trunk. A few papers that he had been working on lay strewn by his side and he closed his eyes for a few moments' rest. As he drifted off to sleep, the air next to his house crackled and fizzed and Bryan, The Commissioner, Langley Von Tinklehorn

Bryan closed his eyes and breathed deeply.

"The beginning and the end of every circle are the same place," he said mysteriously. "The question you need to ask is where do you find yourself? At the beginning? Or at the end?"

"You're right, Bryan-san," said Samuel Nathaniel Daniels, tapping furiously on his InfoTab. "According to my calculations, the apple is about to fall."

Bryan looked at Langley Von Tinklehorn and nodded, Langley looked at The Commissioner and nodded, The Commissioner looked at Samuel Nathaniel Daniels and nodded.

"Friends," said Bryan, bowing slightly. "The TIME has come for ACTION. Let's get the apple!"

With those words, Langley, The Commissioner and Samuel Nathaniel Daniels started to run as *fast* as they could towards HISTORY'S GREATEST SCIENTIST and the apple tree. Bryan bowed once again and began to walk, quite s l o w l y but with a calm confidence into Sir Isaac Newton's garden. Suddenly, on the other side of the garden, the air crackled and fizzed and Gussage St Vincent, Jinxy LaBabbage, Scawby Briggs and Compton all

APPEARED.

Gussage had a tight hold on Compton.

LET ME GO!

Compton yelled.

"QUICK!" cried Gussage. "The apple is about to fall. Get ready to grab it!"

Jinxy and Scawby began to scramble over the grass towards the apple tree.

All the commotion woke Sir Isaac Newton from his blissful afternoon snooze. It would be fair to say that what he witnessed next was completely unexpected. As he opened his eyes, he watched in disbelief as a woman dressed in a furry orange onesie with tight shiny gloves and a pair of see-through boots, a man wearing a tight silver suit and a tiny bowler hat, another HEROIC-looking man with long flowing locks and wearing a long black coat covered in mirrored stars, and two people dressed as pirates ALL charged towards his beloved Flower Of Kent apple tree.

264

He was just about to ask *what* in the name of the Fourth Earl of Southampton was going on when he spotted a small, ten-year-old boy, wearing a silk dressing gown and a pair of wooden sandals, walking purposefully towards him from the distance. The boy had such a look of tranquillity on his face that Sir Isaac quite forgot about anything else that was happening around him. It was then, in this moment of serenity, that he felt a ~bump~ as the apple fell from its branch, hit him smartly on his EXCEPTIONALLY BRAINY bonce and landed on the grass next to him.

Hmmmm,

he thought to himself.

Now THAT *IS* interesting.

As Sir Isaac Newton was coming up with the equation for the LAW OF UNIVERSAL GRAVITATION, Scawby and Jinxy closed in on the apple.

Jinxy made the first move and DIVED head first over the still reclining body of Sir Isaac Newton.

Langley Von Tinklehorn knew that he had ONE chance to stop Jinxy before he got to the apple and so he *launched* himself towards the diving pirate. He CRASHED into him in mid-air and knocked Jinxy into a

HEAP on the FLOOR.

Seeing his chance, Scawby hurdled Sir Isaac Newton but badly misjudged the distance, accidentally kicking the apple and p i n g i n g it across the garden.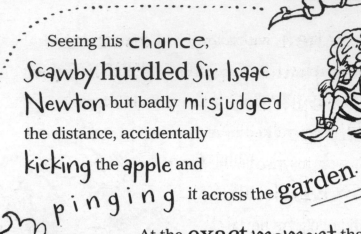

At the exact moment that Scawby attempted his hurdle, Samuel Nathaniel Daniels tripped on a tree root that was poking out of the ground and fell forwards into The Commissioner.

As the full weight of Samuel Nathaniel Daniels fell into her, The Commissioner was catapulted with ENORMOUS speed into Scawby, squashing him flat.

Then, with a level of **peace** and **composure** that made **EVERYONE** think he had **planned it** from the beginning, **Bryan** walked over to the **apple**, **flicked** it with his **foot** high into the air and **caught** it behind his back. As he **did** this, the air around him **crackled** and **fizzed** for a **moment** and his **samurai** clothing was replaced by a **red F. A. R. T. Academy** onesie. *

* The act of grabbing the apple that had hit Sir Isaac Newton on the head had changed the **TIMELINE** once again. One of the results was that Bryan was NO LONGER a samurai master and DIDN'T have his own TV show, which was probably just as well really!

The Commissioner let out a cheer of delight, got up from squashing Scawby and rushed over to Bryan to congratulate him, but a familiar voice shattered The Commissioner's celebration.

Oh, well done, Bryan,

said Gussage St Vincent, still holding tightly on to Compton. Now hand over the apple or you'll NEVER see your friend AGAIN.

Bryan looked at The Commissioner and then at Compton.

DON'T DO IT, BRYAN!

yelled Compton.

Langley, Samuel Nathaniel Daniels, Scawby and Jinxy all got to their feet.

"Quick as you can, there's a good boy," said Gussage. "THE UNIVERSE isn't going to take over itself, you know."

"No, Bryan, NO!" said Compton, shaking his head furiously.

In changing from Bryan-san to plain old Bryan, an awful lot of VERY IMPORTANT information had left Bryan's brain. Unfortunately for all concerned, the ENORMOUS hole that the missing information had left behind had been filled with clouds of doubt and swirling pools of confusion.

Bryan stared blankly at the apple in his hand, not really knowing what to do for the best.

"I'm sorry," he said eventually, looking straight at his

GREATEST FRIEND
IN THE
WHOLE WORLD.

"I don't know what else to do."

Bryan looked at Gussage and tossed the apple to him. Gussage caught the apple in his free hand and held it up in TRIUMPH.

Still holding on to Compton, Gussage tossed the apple over to Scawby.

"You two take the apple back to Fandango's Revenge," he said, a WICKED smile flashing across his lips. "I'll be back in a mo."

Jinxy LaBabbage pushed a button on his W.A.T.CH., the air in the garden crackled and fizzed and he and Scawby DISAPPEARED.

"LET COMPTON GO," shouted Bryan. "You've got what you want."

Gussage thought for a moment.

"Do you know what?" he said, wrapping his arms round Compton so that he could use his W.A.T.CH. and hold on to him. "I've changed my mind. I think I'll keep him. Take one LAST look at your friend, because you'll NEVER SEE HIM

AGAIN. HA HA HA HAAAAA!"
Compton couldn't believe what he was
hearing. There was no way he wanted to
be stuck with Gussage St Vincent for the
rest of his life.

He
suddenly
felt
ANGER
boiling and
bubbling
DEEP
within him.

Before Gussage had a **chance** to use his

W.A.T.CH., Compton **stamped down**

hard on his **foot**. Gussage let out a

great howl of pain

YOWWWEEE!!

but **didn't** let

go of Compton. In fact,

he just grabbed him *even*

tighter around his **chest**.

YOU LITTLE
GREASE BARREL!

he **yelled**. I'll GET YOU for **that**.

But Gussage didn't have a **chance** to do

anything else, because in a **second**,

Compton reached behind him and grabbed

the **W.A.T.CH.** on Gussage's **wrist**. Without

hesitation he started pushing buttons as

hard as he could.

276

WHAT ARE YOU DOING? yelled Gussage. **WHAT is hap—**

Nobody heard the end of Gussage's question because the air in the garden **crackled** and **fizzed** again and Compton and Gussage St Vincent DISAPPEARED.

Chapter 22

Saturday 1st September 1956 (Memphis, USA)

Elvis Aaron Presley admired his beautiful new shoes. He had only just bought them but he *knew* they were PERFECT. He had wanted a pair in this colour for simply ages. He stood in his bedroom, looking at himself in his full-length mirror, and wiggled his hips.

"Man, I *LOVE* these shoes," he said in his soft southern drawl.

Suddenly the air in his room crackled and fizzed and a man dressed as a pirate and a boy in an ancient Roman toga APPEARED out of nowhere.

Chapter 23

708 BCE (Olympia, Ancient Greece)

The crowd that had gathered around the ENORMOUS wrestling square shouted LOUDLY. Two wrestlers were locked in battle but it was the favourite, a big, fat hairy man, who seemed to have the upper hand. He had rolled his competitor onto his back and was sitting on his belly, urging the crowd to CHEER his name. Suddenly, the air in the square crackled and fizzed and two more competitors APPEARED. The crowd started to CHEER even more LOUDLY at this most unexpected turn of events.

Gussage and Compton landed on **top** of
the **two** Greek **wrestlers** and
knocked the favourite off the challenger.
LET GO OF MY W.A.T.CH.!
yelled Gussage, as the pair **rolled**
around the square, before the air **crackled**
and **fizzed again** and they
DISAPPEARED.

Seeing his **chance**, the challenger **jumped** up and **sat** on the **dazed** favourite's **head**. Being a **local lad**, this brought **more CHEERS** from the **crowd**, who **suddenly** *rushed* into the square and pronounced him the **winner** of the **very first wrestling** event at the **Olympic games.**

Chapter 24

Thursday 25th July 2120 (Downing Street, London)

The Prime Minister, Weston LaFell, stood on the steps of number ten Downing Street in his immaculate grey, pinstriped suit and faced the jostling crowd of the world's media. There were cameras and reporters and vloggers all shouting questions at him.

WHAT really happened, Prime Minister?

WHY did you use gravy?

Did the QUEEN know WHAT was going on?

The Prime Minister held up his hands to calm the crowd.

"Please, *please*, let me speak," he said. "There is a PERFECTLY normal explanation for what happened. If you'll *just* let me explain."

As he spoke the air in front of him crackled and fizzed and Gussage and Compton APPEARED.

STOP STOP STOP STOP STOP STOP STOP STOP!

yelled Gussage.

NO! I will NOT let YOU TAKE OVER THE UNIVERSE!

yelled back Compton and the pair continued their **wrestle** through **TIME** and **space**. As they **tussled** and **grappled** on the ground in front of the **Prime Minister**, the **buckle** on Gussage St Vincent's **pirate boot** caught in the **pocket** of the Prime Minister's **trousers**. Gussage's **leg** then *jerked* **suddenly** and **somehow** managed to **rip** the **PM's trousers** **COMPLETELY** **OFF HIS LEGS**.

The air in Downing Street crackled and fizzed and Gussage and Compton DISAPPEARED, leaving the Prime Minister standing in his suit jacket, shirt, tie and a pair of pale blue boxer shorts with the words "mummy's boy" written all over them.

I RESIGN!

he said and went back inside number ten.

Chapter 25

Monday
9th November
(Over 5 Billion Years
in THE FUTURE)

The air **crackled** and **fizzed** and Compton and Gussage St Vincent **APPEARED**, still **grappling**, in the space that had **once** been the **Future Perfect Unit** HQ in **New New London**, but was now **nothing** more than a **HUGE** patch of **scorched, cracked mud**.*

* The patch of scorched, cracked mud had also been the site of London, *New* London, New New *New* London, Mega London, London 4.0, Nodnol and briefly, in the year 3420, a popular aquatic leisure facility after the last of the ice caps melted.

In the sky above them, the
ENORMOUS crimson sun puffed
and ballooned its way into a Red Giant.
The air was hot and dry and before long the
HEAT got the better of Compton and Gussage
and they fell into a dusty HEAP. As they
lay there, struggling to breathe in the
stifling air, they saw the remains of dozens
of ancient rocket launch pads that the
native CYBER HUMANS had used to escape the
Earth's hostile environment
nearly half a billion years earlier.
At that moment, Compton Valance and
Gussage St Vincent were

THE ONLY TWO
LIVING THINGS
ON THE WHOLE
PLANET.

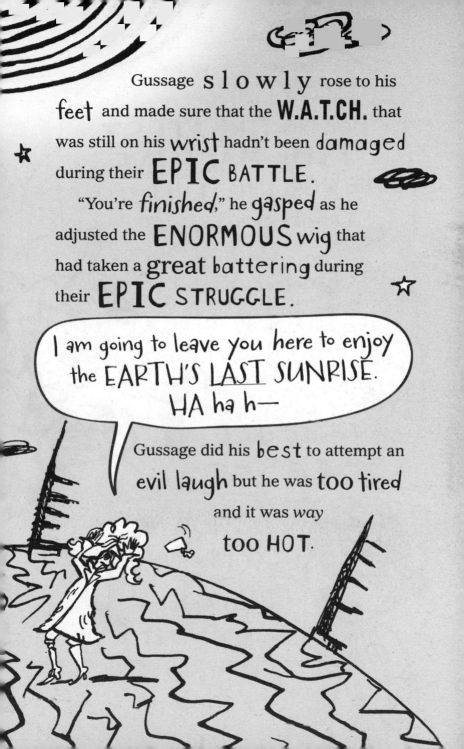

Gussage s l o w l y rose to his feet and made sure that the **W.A.T.CH.** that was still on his wrist hadn't been damaged during their EPIC BATTLE.

"You're *finished*," he gasped as he adjusted the ENORMOUS wig that had taken a great battering during their EPIC STRUGGLE.

I am going to leave you here to enjoy the EARTH'S <u>LAST</u> SUNRISE. HA ha h—

Gussage did his best to attempt an evil laugh but he was too tired and it was way too HOT.

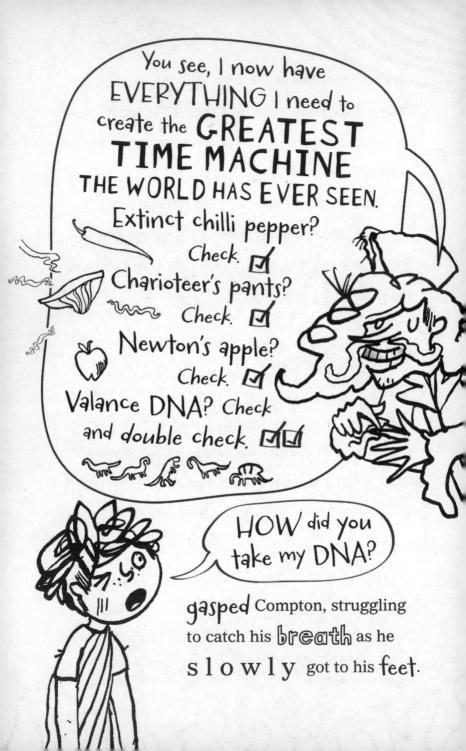

You see, I now have EVERYTHING I need to create the GREATEST TIME MACHINE THE WORLD HAS EVER SEEN. Extinct chilli pepper? Check. ☑ Charioteer's pants? Check. ☑ Newton's apple? Check. ☑ Valance DNA? Check and double check. ☑☑

HOW did you take my DNA?

gasped Compton, struggling to catch his **breath** as he s l o w l y got to his **feet**.

"Well, credit where credit is due," wheezed Gussage St Vincent. "I didn't get your DNA, young Scawby acquired some."

"WHAT?" said Compton. "How?"

"Well, it turns out that a few months ago he did some work experience at the FPU C.A.M.O. DIVISION," said Gussage who, even in the intense HEAT, seemed to have set his face to smug. "Scawby knew exactly where to look for the files and accessed your DNA sequence."

Compton felt his knees go all wobbly. The effort of his millennia-spanning wrestle with Gussage and the tremendous temperature was getting to him. With NO W.A.T.CH., and NO way of letting anyone know WHERE he was, he knew that he would spend his last day on earth BURNING in the year AD 5,000,002,695.

It was **hopeless** – after *all* this **TIME**, Gussage had **WON** and he had **FAILED.**

"Right then," said Gussage. "It's time I **left.** Have **fun!**"

He brushed the **dust** out of his **moustache** but as he did the air around him **crackled** and **fizzed** and Langley Von Tinklehorn

APPEARED

wearing an **FPU** END-OF-TIME protective facemask.

What the...?

said Gussage, momentarily **shocked** by Langley's appearance. "**Langley!**" said Compton, who was almost **too weak** now to **stand.**

Well, well, well, **just you** is it?

Gussage said, regaining his **composure** with a silvery, toothy grin.

You're a bit late and HOPELESSLY understaffed. Do you really THINK that YOU are going to capture ME?

No, said Langley.

YOU are going to be DISTRACTED by ME. You're going to be CAPTURED by HIM.

294

As he spoke the air behind Gussage crackled and fizzed and Bryan APPEARED. In one deft movement, Bryan ≥slapped≤ a pair of laser cuffs onto Gussage's wrists and removed his W.A.T.CH.

NOOOOOOOOOOOOOO!

yelled Gussage as he struggled to free himself from his bonds.

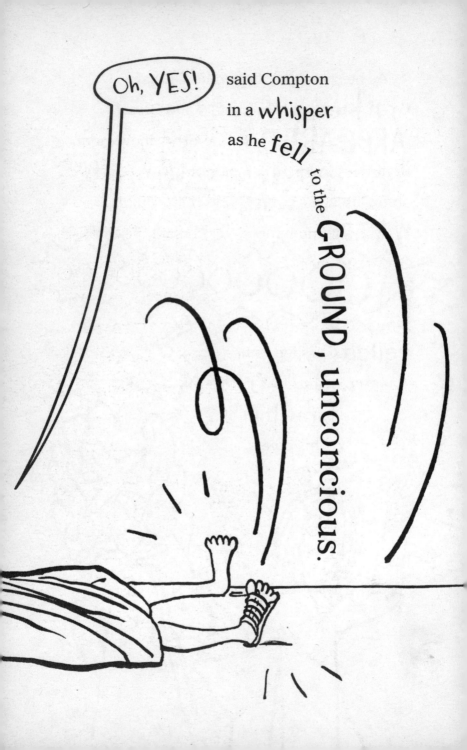

Chapter 26

The End of The Fearless Bandit?

"Now y'all know the rules," said the ROBOT SHERIFF, checking his pocket watch with the town's laser-clock display. "You stand back to back and, on my command, you both walk ten paces. Once you have gone ten paces you may turn and fire."

Compton could feel The Fearless Bandit's back pushing against his.

He looked down at the wobbling custard filling of the pie in his hand. He was ready.

"On your marks, gentlemen," said the ROBOT SHERIFF. "Start walking."

Compton took a step forward and began his s l o w rhythmic walk away from The Fearless Bandit.

He could hear the spurs on his deadly foe's boots =clinking= down the street.

"That's four paces, gentlemen," said the ROBOT SHERIFF. "Ready yourselves."

Compton tensed his hand. He knew he would have to spin round quickly and launch the pie as soon as he had finished walking the ten paces.

"Five, six," said the ROBOT SHERIFF as Compton took another step.

"Seven, eight."

But the **ROBOT SHERIFF** didn't manage to count any further. Compton felt The Fearless Bandit's pie h_it him as he was finishing his ninth step.

The force of it knocked his own pie onto the ground and threw him, spinning onto the floor.

Compton looked at The Fearless Bandit laughing at him on the other side of the street.

HA HA HAAAAAAAAAAAA!

His laughter didn't last long though, as an ENORMOUS dumper truck full of custard APPEARED out of nowhere, right next to him.

Compton looked again and saw that The Fearless Bandit was now completely tied up and couldn't move.

"Hi, Compton," said Bryan, as he jumped down from the driver's seat.

Compton got to his feet and walked over to Bryan. He gave his friend a great BIG hug and then ran across to a lever on the back of the custard truck. He smiled at The Fearless Bandit and pulled the lever. The whole of the back lifted up and dumped enough custard to fill a million pies all over The Fearless Bandit.

GLUG!

GLUG!

{SPLAT!}

SPLAT!

{SPLAT!}

GLUG!

SPLAT!

Bryan and Compton laughed...
Ha ha!
HA HA, HAH
TEE HEE HEE!
Hee hee hee!
(Snort!)
...and laughed.
Guffaw, guffaw!
Heh heh!
HA HA HA, HAH HA HA...
Ha ha!
Ha ha!
Haaah...

"Compton?" said Bryan. "*Compton?*"
Compton s l o w l y opened his
eyes and saw that he was in a white bed,
in a white room. Standing next to the
bed were Bryan, Samuel Nathaniel Daniels,
Langley Von Tinklehorn and The
Commissioner.

W-w-where am I?

said Compton.

It's a secret function on EVERY **W.A.T.CH.** that alerts the **FPU** when that **W.A.T.CH.** is approaching the END of EARTH TIME,

said The Commissioner.

Compton looked blankly

back at the Commissioner.

I DON'T understand.

Look. The earth orbits a sun and like ALL things the sun will eventually die. WHEN the sun dies, the solar system dies and WHEN the solar system dies it will be, I'm afraid, the END of TIME ON EARTH. The alert you triggered told us that the **W.A.T.CH.** Gussage had stolen was DANGEROUSLY close to THAT moment. We were able to get a lock on the EXACT TIME.

It was only thanks to YOU that we managed to STOP him,

said Langley.

If you HADN'T been so brave and put up such a good fight we WOULDN'T have been able to find him.

Thanks for rescuing me,

said Compton to Bryan.

Bryan beamed at his friend.

And NOW you need to rest,

said Samuel Nathaniel Daniels.

You've suffered an EXTREME form of heat exhaustion but the doctors say that you'll be as right as rain in a couple of days.

B—but what about The Fearless? said Compton, sitting up.

They've got EVERYTHING they need to create a TIME MACHINE.

The Commissioner looked at Samuel Nathaniel Daniels and laughed.

You don't need to worry about that. Ancient pirate code demands that the captaincy of the ship passes to the last captain's closest family member. So, unfortunately for The Fearless Crew, with Gussage in jail, their new leader will be Scawby.

"But he *could* make the **TIME MACHINE**," said Compton, still **worried**.

I DON'T think so, **chuckled** Samuel Nathaniel Daniels.

He had the lowest marks EVER recorded in his PHASE THREE: MAKE YOUR OWN TIME MACHINE exam. When it comes to construction and engineering, he's an ABSOLUTE dimwit.

Yes, said The Commissioner, **wiping** a **tear** from her **eye**.

The ONLY way he'll be turning *Fandango's Revenge* into a **TIME MACHINE** is with the help of some kind of SUPER SCIENTIST. I don't think we have ANYTHING to worry about!

And with **that**, Compton fell into a
DEEP sleep and for the **first** time in
months he **didn't dream** about the

COLOSSALLY
MOUSTACHED
FEARLESS
BANDIT.

Chapter 27

Epilogue

Sir Isaac Newton watched as the air in his garden crackled and fizzed and the HUGELY moustached pirate and the ten-year-old boy wearing an ancient Roman toga DISAPPEARED in a ball of FURY. A second later, he heard a weird, screeching alarm cut through the peaceful birdsong that had once again returned to Woolsthorpe Manor.

The Commissioner pushed a few buttons on her **W.A.T.CH.**

"The one Gussage is wearing," she said.

"Time and date?" said Langley.

"10.04 a.m., Monday 9th November, five billion and thirty-one years from now," said The Commissioner.

Langley raised his arms above his head into a classic **CATEGORY FIVE HERO** Pose.

Bryan, he said.

I've got a PLAN but I need your help!

Langley spent the next few minutes filling the others in on his plan. When he finished and everyone was agreed on what they had to do, the air in the garden crackled and fizzed and Bryan, Langley Von Tinklehorn, The Commissioner and Samuel Nathaniel Daniels DISAPPEARED into THE FUTURE.

Sir Isaac Newton was just about to put the **whole** experience down to a **bad** **lamb chop** he'd **eaten** the **night** before, when the air next to him **crackled** and **fizzed** **again** and Scawby Briggs ⋛popped⋚ into view.

Sir Isaac Newton, he said grinning.

I have a little PROBLEM that requires the mind of the cleverest man in HISTORY. It will be your GREATEST CHALLENGE and I think you'll love it. Would YOU like to come with ME?

Acknowledgements

This book is dedicated to my family for their boundless love and unflinching belief that I could do it.

To publish a book takes A LOAD of help from brilliant people. THANK YOU to (in no particular order) all the Usborne peeps especially Becky, Rebecca, Hannah C, Kath, Neil, Hannah R-S, Amy, Megan, Sarah C, Sarah S and the super-talented Lizzie Finlay for having such a clever brain. Thanks as well to Jenny Savill, every single person who I have met and spoken to at a school visit or festival appearance, and last, but definitely not least, EVERY bookseller and librarian. I literally could not have done it without you all.

One question that people ask when they have read one of my books is where my ideas come from. Well, I'll let you into a little secret. If you know where to look, you'll find bits of my life strewn over the pages of the book you're holding right now. I thought I should probably say a few "THANK YOUS" for all the things that have inspired me and helped shape the way I see the world. One big "THANK YOU" needs to go to Kate Tempest, the amazing poet and rapper. When I started writing this I was listening to one of her songs which includes a description of life holding a pistol. I loved that image so much and it reminded me of a gunslinging outlaw, which gave rise in my mind to The Fearless Bandit. The custard pie fights owe themselves to my love of the slapstick comedy films of Laurel and Hardy and Harold Lloyd. I have been a HUGE Elvis fan for almost my whole life and so was thrilled when I could weave him into the story. Ditto Sir Isaac Newton, who is definitely one of my science heroes. When I was about eight I used to love a comic called *Whizzer and Chips*. If you looked carefully you would sometimes see little signs in the strip that said "abolish Tuesdays". I later found out they had been drawn by the cartoonist J Edward Oliver. I was fascinated with those signs and thought they'd make a good chapter title in this book.

Thanks again to YOU for picking this book up and reading it. Reading stories can save your life. Ask me WHY when you next see me and I'll tell you.

OFFICIAL EARTH 1
HERO ASSOCIATION'S
REGULATION HANDBOOK

EVERY KNOWN HEROIC POSE,
FOR EVERY KNOWN HEROIC OCCASION

> SNEAKY STANCES

1. *Stealthy Observing* Pose

History: The oldest and best-known of all the sneaky stances.

Use: For greatest impact utilize nearby objects such as trees, full washing-lines or barrels.

2. *Vertical Shark* Pose

History: Created especially for the FPU Diamond Jubilee Swimming Gala in 2569 by Perivale Greenford.

Use: Perfect for deep-sea posing.

3. The *Elevated Gravy Boat* Pose

History: Rumoured to have been the favoured pose of Queen Victoria to exit banquets without being seen.

Use: Restricted due to difficulty in achieving high speeds.

> EXTREME DANGER

1. *Ecuadorian Action Stations* Pose

History: First used in 2570 by the
Ecuadorian pro-celebrity darts
team. Their 10-0 victory at the
EPC Darts Cup was widely thought
to be due to this cunning pose.

Use: A sharply pointed back toe is essential.

2. *Flying Badger* Pose

History: First used by Flying Badger spotters
in the twenty-fourth century.

Use: Flight direction dependent
on situation. Upside-down-
badgering may cause
seasickness.

3. *Action Pose #8* (French Style)

History: First used during "Le Grand
Bagette Clash" of 2103.

Use: Requires flexibility and an
outrageous French accent.

4. *Intense Hero* Pose

History: The intense hero has no history.
A hero will find themselves assuming
the pose when, and only when,
THE MOST EXTREME DANGER is near.

Use: Do not attempt after eating large
quantities of Formula 1.79.

TRAVEL BACK **IN TIME** and read Compton and Bryan's first three eye-wateringly **EXCELLENT** adventures!

"Funny, clever, brilliant – I love this book
Buy it immediately!" Dermot O'Leary

COMPTON VALANCE

The Most **POWERFUL BOY** in the **UNIVERSE**

BY MATT BROWN

"Funny, clever, brilliant – I love these books!" Dermot O'Leary

COMPTON VALANCE

The **TIME-TRAVELLING SANDWICH BITES BACK**

BY MATT BROWN

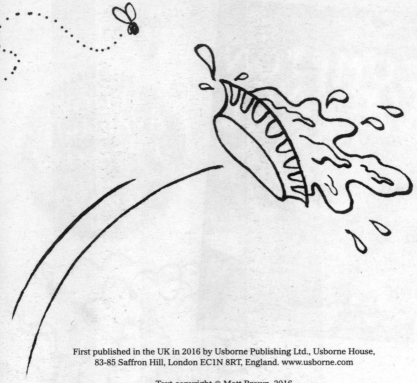

First published in the UK in 2016 by Usborne Publishing Ltd., Usborne House,
83-85 Saffron Hill, London EC1N 8RT, England. www.usborne.com

Design: Hannah Cobley, Neil Francis, and Katharine Millichope.
Editorial: Sarah Stewart and Becky Walker.

The name Usborne and the devices 🎩 🎈 are Trade Marks of Usborne Publishing Ltd.

A CIP catalogue record for this book is available from the British Library.

J MAMJJASOND/16

ISBN 9781474906487 03944/1
Printed in the UK.